Ismael and His Sisters

LOUISE STERN grew up in Fremont, California, the fourth generation born deaf in her family. She is an artist and the author of *Chattering* (Granta, 2010). Her art, which is based around ideas of communication and language, has been exhibited in Geneva, London, Paris, New York City, Madrid, and other places. She lives in London.

ALSO BY LOUISE STERN

Chattering

Ismael and
His Sisters

LOUISE STERN

GRANTA

Granta

First published in Great Britain by Granta Books, 2015

This paperback edition published by Granta Books, 2016

Copyright © Louise Stern, 2015

Louise Stern has asserted her moral right under
the Copyright, Designs and Patents Act, 1988, to be
identified as the author of this work.

A CIP catalogue record for this book
is available from the British Library.

2 4 6 8 9 7 5 3 1

ISBN 978 1 84708 946 5
eISBN 978 1 84708 947 2

Typeset in Bembo by Patty Rennie
Printed and bound by CPI Group (UK) Ltd, Croydon, CR0 4YY

MIX
Paper from
responsible sources
FSC® C020471
FSC
www.fsc.org

*For the Colli Collis and everyone in the village,
and for Omar y Rodolfo.*

Chapter One

The village lay in the south, just beneath the point where the green mountains sloped coarsely down into aridity. Chickens walked in their certain, jerky way along the roads of red dust, and children lay on the concrete of the basketball court in the centre of town as if they were floating on an unfathomable sea. The air was thick with moisture that would hold certainties aloft and free.

In the three cement-block churches; in the orange-yellow beer store that lay near the edge of the jungle, just a few feet away from tens of pink, nearly translucent lizards running over the rough branches of the trees and twenties of shiny black beetles with their wings folded neatly across their backs; in the cool mint-green school; everywhere in town, lips gave flight to swollen words that rose to just beneath the heavens, and accumulated there. It was the same in all the rest of the world.

In the village, talk ran another way as well; it was signed. It moved with the blood through the veins and into the arms and hands. The antennae of a butterfly were made of crossed thumbs, its wings by flapping fingers. This language was something you could see, something you could feel, like you saw and felt the real butterfly.

For death: the finger across the neck, the eyes turned up, the tongue creeping out as something left the body. The expression on the face close to the one on the Virgin of Guadalupe, but you could feel it more in yourself. It wasn't distant. Then the palms down by the waist, and sweeping away. The infinite secret of death was there in the sign. It was not explained away nor veiled. But you understood that the same void, fear, and surrender coalesced around death for other people, and that made it easier. It helped things come together in you.

All this Ismael only understood when he left the village.

There were deaf people in the big city. There were deaf people all over the world. But not as many as were grouped together in the village, and the language was not shared with everyone.

The people in the village did not rush like fire ants to work, to the supermarket, to deposit pennies into a hole; when one had food, all had food. When a few could not hear or talk, all learnt the language of the deaf.

Some could sign better than others; but for all, talk turned to gesture and back to talk easily. The house of the

2

tailor Chabelo was always filled with people and gossip. When Ismael climbed the long flight of concrete steps up the small hill and into the shade of the tile-floored house by the basketball court, everyone stopped speaking Mayan – without needing to think about it – and continued with their hands.

—Man live house next street here, bent back, he drink drink much last night, he take little boy slingshot, he draw back, shoot shoot rock there Teodoro whisker chin! Teodoro whisker chin bleed bleed! Bent back man now in jail him.

And Ismael always had to put in something of his own.

—That man bent back, he crazy!

Often, the people who could hear used the language of the deaf among themselves. They knew it as well as their own, and there were many times when it felt more comfortable.

—Point there, come here! Eat now! Finger shake more play play. Papa said me tell you. Papa whip you!

When Mama's body assumed authority, became imperious and brutal; when the muscles in her shoulders hunched and bunched, her arms extended around the chest, her rigid fingers outspread and jerky, the child knew she would have to stop crouching on the top of the pile of red dirt that would be used to even out the ruts in the

3

street and come home for the night, to wash, eat, and sleep.

Because of all of this, there was not much difference between the deaf and the hearing in the village; a head turned more quickly towards a loud noise or the radio, a storyline followed more closely on the nightly telenovelas, eyes somehow more awake to the movements in the world and in the body; that was all.

There were other places like the village in the world, but only a very few, and they were fragile.

As Ismael arrived in the big city with its black asphalt roads that lay sticky in the glaring sun, the bordering walks where demanding feet were pulled along in straighter lines, he stumbled on the uneven cobblestones of the roads around the central square, different to the dirt roads of the village, but he persevered. He asked a pretty lady in a pink skirt where the market was.

—Fingers against palm, brush-away, brush-away.

He said it again and again, but she did not answer, and her flat eyes burned into anger, pushing Ismael to the next person, where he was received the same way. He turned into a small, rocky alley and then a narrower one, burrowing deeper into the unfamiliar city where suddenly all others were cut off from him, but found neither the market nor anyone who would take the question.

As the desperate night fell, he saw the absence of chatter

from the sweaty, pungent limbs and torsos all around. It only came from the mouth here. That was why nobody understood him, he finally saw.

He pressed the stub of a broken pencil onto paper to make the shaky lines that joined into *Mercado*, one of the few Spanish words he knew, and at last a man in pointed snakeskin boots told him where. There he found work; but now he saw that if he wanted to stay here, he would not be any part of things.

Back in the village Ismael had been king; all raised hands to him when he left his house in the morning, and in the evening all crowded to sit next to him when the men sat in the soft shadows in front of the biggest store and raised a beer to another sweltering day gone. When the cartel came to the village, Ismael had been the only one who made money, but knew how to stay far enough away from the narcos. The only one who built a beautiful house with his pesos and didn't put it all up his nose, down his throat, or into the pockets of women who spent it on lipstick and high heels. The house was in the centre of town and except for the original lean-to that had belonged to their parents, it was stone, with a corrugated metal roof. Most of the other houses were lean-tos or concrete boxes.

Ismael's two sisters, Cristina who couldn't stop talking and silent Rosie, came to him for everything.

But the village had driven him out and he could not go back.

So in the big city, Ismael sat intently smoothing all of the rivulets in the cement into utter unadulterated wholeness of grey while talk of the narcos, death, cocaine, women, *pobres*, *cervezas*, tequila, pulque, children, PRI, PAN, the possibility of work in the Costena plant, and where the best tacos barbacoa were to be found fluttered as panicky as moths above him.

Back in the village, his elder sister Rosie rocked in her hammock in the lean-to behind the house Ismael had built and then departed, her eyes on the discolorations of the wall in front of her. The marks spread in the same irregular blotches as the brown, mottled stains that had come onto Rosie's cheekbones with age, beneath her laugh lines. Her feet, as small, square and soft as bread rolls, protruded gently from the hammock.

His younger sister Cristina sat on the stoop out front in her traditional Maya dress, bright embroidered flowers around the square collar and hem and beneath that, lace to her plump knees. The white bodice swung easy around her thick body, catching the rare movements in the sultry air. Her hungry eyes twitched busily, ready to fix on any whiff of rancid or fresh information that came across the heavy air. Had Estevanya finally cleaned up the patch of dirt in front

6

of the house where she lived alone with three babies by three different men, as they had said at the tortilleria that morning? For as long as anyone could remember, her yard had been thickly carpeted with deodorant cans, staring teddy bears with matted fur, broken tricycles, upended plastic fuel jars, and bloated diapers that the dogs with prominent ribcages fed on.

The thought of Ismael was with both sisters. Where was he, who would he be out of their sight? They had only known life with him. But he was gone, and there was the courtyard to rake and the voluptuous tomatoes to water; and the evening meal to cook and eat.

After that, sleep would come, as silence did.

Fifty years before, when Rosie was born, the priest, who had come down to the village from Mexico City and did not understand the language of the deaf, said it was their father's mother who had brought the curse of deafness down onto the heads of the family. There were many deaf people in the village and everyone was related one way or the other. But no immediate relatives were like Rosie, or, later, like Ismael or Cristina.

But even from Ismael and Cristina, even from the other deaf in the village, Rosie was different.

The inflammation started in Alondra's chest, not long

after she married the grandfather of Ismael, Rosie and Cristina. She worked all day washing other people's clothes to feed her children, to buy them shoes and send them to school. Her twinkle-eyed husband lay in his hammock, except when he was pushing up against other women behind the small medical clinic. The feelings bloated her. The distrust when he was drunk and stupid. The anger when he took the coins she had got selling cilantro to the other villagers and salted away in a jar, and bought food with her money because he had not been looking for work. The hesitation when he asked and asked her to promise him that they would always be together.

The children grew up and the parents became old and wrinkled, but the inflammation did not shrink. It formed a gaseous bubble that exploded into her veins. Some of it hissed out of her body, entered the sky and spread like a blemish. Later, the congealing weight of the molecules finding each other again sank back down into their father's mother and expanded into every curve and fold of her body and soul, and one day as she walked two hours out with her husband to work in the corn fields, the inflammation burst completely.

She shot him once in the groin with his own pistol in the old lean-to in the fields, where a ragged purple hammock with rust-coloured stains still swayed. But she did not kill him, and she did not have any more bullets.

By his strong forearms, he dragged himself back to the village, like a lame, engorged dog. He left a snail's trail of blood, and the uncompromising purity of the stars emerged above and shone down onto him. When they faded again and the sky became light, and the viscera spread behind him all the way to the old lean-to, he twisted up and died just outside the first house in the village.

Nobody ever saw or heard of Alondra again. But the only grandchildren born to the family could not hear or speak. The priest said it was because talk, confession, forgiveness and cleansing could have saved their grandmother, but she had forsaken the Word for blood. And so her grandchildren did not have the Word. More than that, they grew up with the story always around them, pinching and buzzing like a large, persistent mosquito. Every time one of the children did something puzzling to the rest of the villagers, the story was turned to for explanation.

The story was everywhere around them. It awakened their passions even as it told them that they were helpless to the eruptions of the soul that ran in their blood.

The very first grandchild of the family, christened Rosina in the Catholic church by the basketball court but always called Rosie, had a haze of stillness around her from birth that divided her from the lethal ruckus of the world.

She did not cry when she first came out of their mother, and less sound came from her than from anyone else in the village. Even through her hands, little came from her.

She sat where you put her, and moved slowly and seldom; she helped diligently; she laughed long and hearty. She liked best to be by the side of her family.

The world of opinions that masqueraded as realities did not exist for Rosie. She lived only in her body and what she could see, taste, feel, and grasp. The wavering but loyal companions that lay inside her were so much more constant than anything outside herself, except for the liquid line of the horizon. Occasionally something pierced, but she pushed it out fast to join the heaps of rubbish that lined the roads. When she stood in the queue at the tortilleria and saw all the women gossiping about husbands, lovers, and children, Rosie thought they tossed their feelings out like she tossed the slimy wash water into the courtyard of their house. Those organs they drew up from inside their bodies landed on the road with a splat, like pigs' intestines after butchering. The women stood callously away when other people's innards flew past their noses.

All the small children in the village came in from the sun to nestle next to Rosie's quiet bulk for some protected minutes.

Her brother and sister watched over Rosie even more

after their parents died when Rosie was thirty-five. Their parents had gone to line up for hours with the other Maya under the harsh sun in the central square of a bigger town, to press their thumbs onto the papers of bloodshot government officials sitting behind folding tables under the lavish shade of a peeling colonial building with fuchsia bougainvillea growing up the pillars, and receive a few doled out pesos in exchange. On the way back to the village, the parents of Rosie, Ismael and Cristina had been sitting in purple and pink rubber chairs in the back of an old Chevy truck, when it went off the road into flames.

But when Ismael got into one of his spiels, he made fun of Rosie.

—Sister there never talk no one! Sister there Rosie-old her, mind different, mind flat on-on-on left, flat on-on-on right. Leave sister there alone, that her Rosie-old, sister there little bit crazy!

Cristina could not stop herself pinching, scratching, and taking bites from Rosie when there were no tales around town to distract her from the molten boredom, and it cocooned slowly, crushingly, and completely around her like a boa constrictor. People sat. The rocky brown of the road turned into the dust brown of the dogs sleeping in the sun. The children jumped through the fullness of the air as the adults never did. Ants covered the corpse of a banana, scraping away everything they could from the fruit into their tiny bodies.

Rosie weathered it all. In the huge, gleaming eye of her mind she saw the two trees outside town, in the field she liked best to chop food for the cows in. One tree was covered with three-pointed thorns that somersaulted over its trunk and enclosed its branches. It resembled the porcupines and sea urchins that Rosie had seen on the television. Its spindly branches wavered. Often they swerved suddenly towards the ground, as if they were not sure they wanted to leave it.

Opposite the spiky tree grew a very different one. The trunk of this tree was muscular and satiated. It became stems that stayed faithful to their mother. They reached up unhurriedly. The branches were broad. You would be able to rest your whole body on their ample girth and let your arms and legs hang over contentedly, as they would over the body of a satisfying lover.

Its knots were the perfect size and distance apart to be footholds, and the places where its lowest branches met were good to hoist up on.

Rosie had seen both the spiky tree and the strong one grow bigger and taller over the years, but they still made her incredulous and she never fully settled on which one to believe.

One went before the other. And then something brought you back to the other, again.

The day Ismael left town, the strong tree reached into Rosie, the trunk rose up through her chest, and sturdy branches spread into her limbs. And she knew that Ismael would find his way, and that he would be back one day. It did not matter what had gone before he left.

The next day, it was the spiky tree that came into Rosie's mind; but she was further away from Ismael's disappearance then and did not look closely enough to see that Ismael would bring even more chaos back than he had left with.

Everything that was built up in Rosie, and present in Ismael to a lesser degree, had shattered in Cristina and leaked from her. It was evident from the moment she came shrieking abrasively into the world, her face obscured by a gaping, bottomless mouth.

The fecund seed pods and ovaries of the plants in the village split open and haemorrhaged acidly onto the dirt when Cristina was born. The fields dried up. Clouds of ravens descended on the lonely, bare trees to guard the branches, so black that neither eyes, beaks, nor bodies could be seen; only blots hunched against the hulking blue of the big sky. The birds stayed and stared until the baby Cristina was washed and, for shock of the cold water on her delicate, febrile skin, stopped crying. Then they left the earth, disappearing into the comfort of the never-ending billows where not much that was definable could ever follow them, in spite of vain efforts.

A disproportionate share of the destructive, sorrowful, human part of the soul that usually finds enough relief in the bottle or the Iglesias not to dominate writhed into Cristina. It was not to be soothed, no matter what Cristina fed its ravenous appetite, nor when she tried to starve it into obedience.

Other girls in the village made flower chains in the field past Susana's hut; Cristina sat with a heap of thorns and pricked herself, glossy globules of red bubbling from her flesh. When her squat, calm father walked her to school, she insisted on drawing a stick up above her head and striking every house, fence, or cement block they passed.

There were remissive periods when it sank back underground and solidified. Then laughter skulked into Cristina and seduced her entirely, and she knew irrevocably there was a God. These were months when she never left Rosie's side and a perfect alchemy of flavours came into her cooking, salt and sweet, citrus and smoke; when she, Ismael, and Rosie went gratified into their hammocks at night. The stars glowed down from the soft blackness of the immeasurable sky and the far-away clear radiance filled them up. The insecure apprehension that so often disturbed her came into its proper place alongside everything else around them, and it all crystallized into something to hold on to, balancing in the air in a droplet of graceful synchronization.

Just as they were lulled into believing that the blessed would last always, the seesaw went up and down, banging on the ground with none of the former gentleness, and they fell into the pinholes of doubt, spun around and around like clothes in their washing machine, then came into womb warmth for a few short instants before they were pushed through the opening again and landed back among the recognizable souvenirs of banal existence, to try to get on with it without much more respite.

Cristina with her vicious anxiety that could not be named; placid Rosie; and Ismael, in between.

The only brother in the middle of two sisters, Ismael moved golden and easy between the outer world and what lay within. If something troubled him, he had only to allow it to dissolve, liquefy, and become part of the world again. The story of their grandparents did not touch Ismael throughout his youth, although it would invade his adult life as it did his sisters'.

He ran slowly and happily, threw a ball to the other children to be hit back with a stick, found solace in the sweep of a girl's breast. Like most boys in the village, he carried a rubber and wood slingshot around his neck and used it to knock birds out of the trees, dragonflies from the sky, and lizards off the comforting heat of walls; anything else that stirred from the quiet could surely be taken care of the same way. He was the only one who could appease Cristina when her turmoil came to the surface, and he was steady next to Rosie. When adolescence came, the red of aggressive hurt came into the other boys' eyes but not into Ismael's, not till years later. He told jokes energetically and sat staring off into the distance like an iguana. For a long while, he plodded steadily. He had established the peripheries, determined the order of his day, decided that he was brother and friend. He planted corn alongside all the other men until the cartel came to town, and after a different cartel took over and decided the village was not essential to them, Ismael went back to the corn without regret. Three cows were tied up next to Ismael's house, more than anyone else in the village had, and he fed them well.

When he sat on the front stoop next to his father's bulk, beside his mild eyes like the cows' and his wide, brown face with the large triangular nostrils atop the barrel chest and the bow legs in the leather sandals, and smelled his father's smell of salty sweat and yeasty beer, Ismael knew before his father opened his arms that he would be asked to look after his sisters always. And that of course he would.

His father's swarthy, hairy arms and sausage fingers started with the ground, and stopped with the ground.

—You flat-palm down near ground, raise-up tall above ground; Cristina-big same; Rosie-old same. Flat-palm reach into space ahead; not know what there. Shrug. Cristina-big up and down, sharp peak, down down down crash next day; wave wave possible. Rosie-old flat, on-on-on left, flat on-on-on right, same same same. You eyes look-watch point-her, look-watch point-her, flat-palm reach into space far far far ahead . . . calm . . . calm . . . down till ground.

His father carved the space around himself into materiality where he could, and indicated the tremble of uncertainty where it lay. This was how the language of his children worked; and this was the first language he had known, growing up in the village. This was the stuff of shape and form, of landscape and emotion, of the things that could not be caught in the loose net of swollen words. The things that stayed always in you, had a shape in your body, and from which you could physically orient yourself in the world around you. But often this way of placing yourself in your situation made the knowledge of all that could not be controlled immediate and agonizing.

Ismael told his father before he died,

—I look-watch them-two.

And he meant it, and he did it. It reassured others, that Ismael always did what he set out to do. That was why, when he stopped doing it, it made such a sharp tremor under the village.

But the tug of gravity on the guts can be potent; it can reshape the innards. The damage done by the natural disasters of the soul could be steadily and regularly restored, as the cells of the body were and as the land was.

Other times chaos was pulled up to meet already present electricity, and the terrain turned into badlands that could never be regrown or even metamorphosed. A place where only aliens and fiends could exist, for evermore; a bone-dry place where the wind blew through straight and harsh.

Cristina knew it better than she knew anything else. Ismael never saw it, but he came closer to it than anyone had ever thought he would. It was Rosie who understood it.

Chapter Two

Village life drummed a regular cadence. The morning saw women with coloured plastic bowls filled with corn on their heads on their way to feed one of the two huge iron machines that ground the kernels into dough to be made into tortillas over the cooking fires, and then the women swept and washed till it was time to prepare the main meal in the late morning or early afternoon. The men took ropes and machetes to the thickets to hack down vines and weeds to feed the cows with, or they were in the fields to press kernels of corn into the soil in the same way that their grandfathers' grandfathers' grandfathers had.

Every house had a well or a plastic reservoir of rainwater, and pails were thrown down to bring up the transparent liquid for cooking, bathing, and cleaning.

All day long when they weren't at school, the children jumped off their front stoops, clambered onto the steps again, and jumped off; any nearby adults caught them in their arms and twirled their rotund legs high in the air, and they were as free as they would ever be. The old ones lay in their hammocks inside the houses, watching masked, roaring wrestlers bang into the ropes and boomerang off to slam into each other again on the television, or fed the chickens with stray bits of corn. Some shivered and wrapped themselves up tighter in whatever sheets and blankets they had; it was colder than they remembered it in their youth, they agreed.

The weight of just washed clothes, embroidered tortilla cloths, and rags scoured in the concrete tubs outside every house pushed the washing lines that crisscrossed the entire village close to the ground. Water dripped from the clothes, and the circles of moisture stretched out on the dirt, shrunk little by little in the sun, and disappeared.

After the washing, sweeping, and cooking were finished, the women stood by their hammock looms, watching television whilst zigzagging the wooden triangle in and out of the coloured threads.

Some went to the big city for spells of time, to clean one of the houses or hotels there and bring the money back to their families in the village. One cousin of the siblings had gone to the United States and sent money faithfully, but while he was away, his wife had a baby by another man and so Jairo never came back.

Occasionally people came to study the villagers and

their language. Cristina told stories about all of them, and framed photos of one or other of them hung in many houses in the village alongside the family photos and Guadalupe. There was one hearing man, named with a circled finger over an eye for his spectacles, who had taken all the deaf people to the market in the nearby town, bought them tacos, and let them choose one thing each for him to buy – Cristina had bought a pair of white plastic heart-shaped sunglasses. The villagers nodded approvingly when Spectacles was brought up; but not so another woman,

—flat-palm pat down, Shorty,

who stayed in her dank hut all day long and refused all food offered her by the villagers. A constant stream of pesos went from her pocket to her favourites in the village – Margherita in the green house across from the basketball court, who had the phone, and Abstencio who ran the store where you could get batteries. Neither Margherita nor Abstencio were deaf.

Shorty was seduced by the Spanish they knew and thought these two were smart and honest, but they and their friends told her sob stories about their poverty and their sick children and got money off her, and the beer they bought with it drew them into a daily stupor which they shared with Shorty, lying on her unmade, grubby bed in her dirty room.

Everyone's favourite was the first one to come, called Beardy. He came back again and again, and brought his wife with him; he took photographs and films that he sent to everyone; he had built the basketball court for them, but he had not been seen for years.

The crunch of salt or sweet enticed people to the three stores all day long. There were always foil-wrapped packets dropped off by white trucks from the city, and if there was a baseball game or school event, Juan-Deafy would be there with his blue wheeled cart loaded with clear bags of crispy orange cheese tubes to pour Buffalo hot sauce over and his horn on a rope around his neck to squeeze for the hearing people.

Sometimes if someone had butchered a pig, there would be brown wraps of rich pork crackling on the counter in the biggest store, grease spreading dark on the bags.

Cristina cooked the noon meal; her lentil and ground pumpkin seed empanadas were Ismael's favourite, with fresh green tomato salsa spooned over. He also loved eggs from their chickens, scrambled with some of the cilantro Rosie grew in the blue pail out front and lots of salt and tortillas. For the evening meal, the sisters often went to the store for packets of instant noodles or flour tortillas to fill with ham and cheese slices and cook over the fire. Susana came with her two children for supper a few times a week while her

22

husband was away in the city cleaning toilets. Susana's little boy David loved his food. He finished eating first and then he watched everyone else's plate. You could not help but spoon some of your food into his bowl so you could see him grab it and chomp with his small square teeth. He upended the bowl so the last of the juices ran straight into his tummy.

Breakfast was leftovers from the noon meal, eaten sitting on low wooden stools around the fire. Plastic bowls swayed from wood platforms attached to the roof of the lean-to, in them the remainder of ingredients and meals guarded by a piece of embroidered cloth and stored away from the greedy animals. Ladles and spoons hung from wires wrapped around the posts of the lean-to, and more plastic bowls topped the poles beneath the roof. Washing and cleaning rags hung from a rope strung loosely, and a pale green length of sheeting flew in the air in the entrance to the lean-to from the dirt courtyard.

There was a bus to the city every morning; to catch it, you had to wake up in the dark and sit on the old concrete bench by the broken down playground until its bright head-lights made openings in the darkness, the grey gathering and settling either side. After it left, whoever had been keeping the passenger company stayed on the bench a while, watching the darkness plug the area where the bus had been, then it would envelop them too on their way back to their hammock to sleep until the materialization of specks of dust drifting in shards of light. Without clocks, only light and dark pushed you staggering forward.

All day, trucks and cars rumble-bumbled slowly over the potholed dirt roads and through the oppressively damp air, and old women seated in rope chairs in the back of the trucks waved queenly in greeting to people they knew in the town.

People slept or swung in their hammocks. Dogs trotted a safe distance apart but aware of each other, head and tails held high, turning back home to lie in their usual spots in the sun when they realized nobody was hunting today. Small paths enclosed by trees led off the road, through the jungle to spots where people cut firewood, and children on bi-cycles rode up some of them, to places where they could make their own rules and forget about their mothers back in the houses, sweeping and scolding.

Far into the jungle, beyond the trodden paths and the spots where axed firewood had left stumps poking up like rotten teeth, even beyond the stones pushed together and plastic bags tied overhead to make houses imagined up by the children, past the extinguished fires which had been the original clarifying of the dark for pairs of infatuated lovers – nobody has ever been more beautiful than you, and here, finally, is the way out, this warm crook of an exquisite neck where I sink my suffering – the loam temporarily absorbed the pain, joy, and hunger spilt onto it.

Under the costume of these eternal seeming days is the inner rhythm that begins in the core of the earth, and cannot be yoked.

It drove Ismael, Cristina, and Rosie to a fiesta in a nearby town one evening.

By luck and chance, Cristina had been successfully herded along that week. She was diverted by a transform-ation in the fortunes of Estevanya, the woman with the junkyard outside her house and the fatherless children. Estevanya had been deeply shamed by the priest telling her in the street that the time she spent on tittle-tattle outside the biggest store in town should have been directed into cleaning her house and comforting the naked children always in tears.

Clothes now hung on the line outside Estevanya's rented one-room concrete-block house. Although a baby-pink capped Rexona deodorant can and a plastic container of Acirrico chilli and lime seasoning were still caught fast in the tangle of vines that ran up her wire fence, Cristina had seen five sacks of rubbish being burnt behind the house, the bitter smoke spreading all over the village like purifying incense.

And a river of words had washed Estevanya clean the previous evening; she had told an eagerly assembled group outside the church of the impossibility of her ever finding a man again after her past carelessness, and of how hard it was to keep all in order without one.

The admission had brought Cristina even more relief than it had Estevanya. As she waited with Ismael and Rosie for the Volkswagen van that would take them to the fiesta, the familiar encumbrance had left her distended limbs; her eyes lifted from the ground at her feet and looked ahead again. Ismael and Rosie saw it and, in their distinct ways, they noted it as they had so many times before.

Other groups of worshippers gathered around their separate luminosities, the one by the store where the drinkers sat, and the one in the church.

Neidi, who lived next door to Estevanya, stood some way apart from the others, not of either group but easily welcomed into both. She was not voracious for any talk. Her luxuriant flesh absorbed it all; and without knowing it, Cristina was envious.

The van came. Ismael sat between his two sisters in the back seat, one arm around each. Bright pink lipstick covered Cristina's compressed mouth, and there was peacock blue above Rosie's tranquil eyes. Both were in flowered pastel dresses from the stack of crinkled white plastic bags, saved from the shops in the big city, filled with their clothes, and stacked in the lean-to.

Concrete-block houses with square windows through which you saw hammocks heavy with the tumours of bodies, huts roofed with palm fronds, a store with a blue and white Bimbo bread sign above the mostly empty metal racks and children smeared in red dirt standing in the doorway became visible in the headlights, and were gone.

They came to the town of the fiesta; the central square dressed up for the night in ribbons of crêpe paper and coloured lights, and corridors of bicycle carts selling fried potatoes to eat with hot sauce, pieces of papaya and pineapple to sprinkle with the burnt orange of chilli powder, fluorescent green, orange, blue, and pink coconut candy, churros, rum cocktails in plastic cups fogged with moisture, and beer.

Cristina stumped determinedly through the pleasures into the square.

People crowded tight into it, driven there by the same unnameable impulse as the siblings. The fierce young girls dancing were fenced in, and men thrusting with bravado pushed the drunks away. On the benches, under the indolent yellow lights, were the foggy-eyed old people with the small children, sitting and watching longingly, and in the middle was everyone else.

27

At the far end of the square was the temporary stage where the men with their guitars and black hats were warming up. The sign for concert, party, or night of traditional dance was one open hand over heart, the other hand leading like you led a dance, your body moving in that same rhythm. Ismael, Rosie, and Cristina knew the beat well.

Ismael settled his sisters onto a bench near the glossy overhanging leaves of the trees, for, he suddenly saw, they were grey-haired older ladies. Rosie placed her hands formally in her lap, one holding the other safe, and beside her Cristina's acute eyes scanned the crowd for more feed to top up Estevanya's repentance.

Riding the currents of the air around them were flying, invisible sacs containing details people thought had to be told, but which pushed apart their corporeal selves and the shiver of sublime chaos within each one. They drifted through the air and irritated each of them with an occasional reminder; but it was ignored.

Here, everyone lived close enough to the village to know about the deaf. Their eyes met those of Ismael, Cristina, and Rosie, and the man understood when Cristina pointed at the lime-green section of the ice cart for paper cones for herself and Rosie, drawing pesos from the small flower-embroidered drawstring bag in her pocket, made for her by her sister.

Across the square, Ismael set his bottle on his outstretched knee and relaxed his sloping shoulders and his elbows, one on each leg. His barrel chest was ornamented by a heavy gold chain and his back rounded as he settled into being a man at a party, domesticity forgotten. His slanted eyes looked around, his nostrils budding out from the stem of his long, straight nose above wide, thin lips.

Cristiano, who came in and out of their house all day long so he could lie in a different hammock to his own or borrow a cardboard tube to shake oranges out of the tree with, walked past Ismael and his eyes were hard and brilliant, as Ismael had not seen them before. A wide gold chain hung around his thin child's neck. He did not say hello to Ismael, so intent was he on staying right behind his school friend. Their jeans pulled up high with new leather belts and their hands deep in their pockets, they scrutinized all as they moved quickly through the crowd.

Something close to anonymity fell onto Ismael, and it felt refreshing and welcome on his skin. He turned his head so that he could not see Rosie's gentle, full body or Cristina's taut, bulky one.

Another woman, with calves like a capon's and a muscular bulge to her inner thighs, and brilliant emerald-green eyes; she was the one Ismael wanted to look at. He had first seen her a month or two before, at the last fiesta in this town, and she had not left his mind or his body since. He knew she would be here.

Ismael's first wife, Flat-face, had been deaf. She still lived in the village, married to Juan-Deafy with the horn around his neck. She cooked all day for the children Juan-Deafy's first wife had left behind when a huge, round ball grew in her face and ate her up. The thick, stinking blood had come from Flat-face every month for years, and Ismael had told her to go. And after that, his parents had died and there were his sisters.

Sometimes women swinging around poles surprised him in his dreams, and he met them in the big city, shaking the hot, salty smell off on top of the cardboard boxes and pieces of broken glass in the rubble of the back roads after he was finished.

But never before had a woman made his insides splinter into liquid, like the sticky dark brown substance leaked by a crushed insect. Since the first time he had seen her, the dregs of her had settled in him and had been hardening again, like a scab.

He finally saw those calves moving slowly in front of the policemen with their machine guns at the ready, in the waxy, sallow light that slopped out into the plaza from a street lamp in the far corner. He looked away fast for fear of not being able to if he looked any longer, but his body knew just where she was standing. When enough time had risen around him to fill the cracks and make him feel he was safe, he looked at her again. Even from many feet away and even after seeing her only once before, he recognized how the curls in her hair became wirier by her ear and how that piece to the left of her widow's peak always came loose from its tight ponytail. And there were those perceptive green eyes he wished for endlessly.

Underlying all of them at the fiesta and underlying the black was the animate. It descended and then overspilled decadently, nearly going past the black; it reacted, it told living things what to do. Then it forgot their existence and bubbled down in its own redness, then up, up, up just to the bottom of the black, a wisp of smoke up through persuasively, and there were feet too, deliciously crusty, and above the feet the heart beating, beating like a pendulum, like a hand waving urgently from behind fire, the heart where lived humours and tempers that resonated to the song of the red, soon, soon, soon, the song was a catalyst in their hearts, but for now the red receded, below, below the black where only animals with their unfiltered intuition could see.

It had touched Ismael; solid Ismael. It returned him to the straits his grandmother Alondra had known, and the narratives he had grown up with told him how to understand. The world and the land spun and swayed around him, wavering from delicacy and up into the undeniable; and it brought Ismael with it.

Rosie saw it, as she saw everything.

The green-eyed woman leant against the concrete wall, hands behind her back, her ankles crossed above her tinny azure-blue high heels with rhinestones around the rectangular buckles. Ismael saw that her eyes were cautious and as glittery as her shoes. Two men were next to her, one in a sequinned baseball cap, his neck bull-thick with a stupidity and arrogance that Ismael knew well. The other raised his head and Ismael saw a strange, reptilian yellow and green eye next to a normal brown eye. The shaky lines of prison tattoos ran up both arms and the firmer lines of professionally tattooed scorpions began on his forearms and ended on both hands. That snake eye was pitiless and it dug a permanent place for itself in the minds of Ismael and his sisters.

Ismael did not know where the woman's emerald eyes went; her eyes stayed first on the people close to her and then ones further away, examining, summing up, moving on. He wanted to know; and the eyes landed on Ismael and rested on him a long while, and their potential and vibrance made him brave. The men had walked away somewhere.

Ismael wanted to know the secret of these eyes, and he walked to her.

The little finger and thumb of his hand became a beer bottle upended into his mouth, and with a forefinger pointing at her, Ismael asked if she would like a drink.

She nodded. Ismael put his hand into his pocket for pesos, and it shook.

Two beers came out of the vendor's blue and white cooler. He stood against the wall next to her, and the liquid slid down both of their throats, dislodging worries and guilt. The hard coating of her eyes vanished, and Ismael felt his own eyes come unlocked and something grow fully loose in his chest; was it mirrored in her, could it be mirrored?

He pointed to the dance floor, and again she nodded. Her body moved next to his and he knew his emotion was reflected in the shared rhythm and the warm, rosy scent of her flesh, and he was glad it was not the bright, revealing day but the concealing night. She spun, her red skirt making an aureole around her, and then she came back to him.

All above them, sap invisibly crossed into a mantle of wattage that, if you followed it hand over hand, arm over arm, would have made a way for you through flesh, scale, fur, chlorophyll, all down through the heat to the timeless foment of the bottom.

Her small hand stayed in his as they danced and she did not take it back.

But thick hands, the fingers broad and spread like the

33

legs of a crab, slapped down onto his back and he saw that they belonged to the man in the sequinned baseball cap who had been near her. They wrenched him away from her and slammed him against a wall.

Fear entered him when, in the instant that his head cracked against the concrete, he saw that the tautness that had grown in the night was so strong that it ran onto Rosie's body on her bench by the trees. The veins in her languid throat stopped hiding and came forward into sinewy tension, and her skin yellowed to pastiness, the spots and lines joining the veins in prominence.

The green-eyed woman moved away from him and what had sprung up between them disappeared even more quickly than it had come. At its desertion, the newly released dregs in his chest tightened again, and crackled with the new vigour. It was tinder rubbing together to make a spark that was sucked into Ismael's intestines, where it met and ignited the soot of discontent that always rested there. A line of dazzling rage burned itself through and dangled down to feed into Ismael's heart.

He bucked off the man; they were now in the middle of a ring of staring, hungry people, and combustible shards from the subterranean appeared to all. The woman he had dreamed of since he had seen her averted those eyes, now clamped up again, and moved out of his sight. In her place,

Ismael saw the relentless steel mouth of a gun raised at him.

Ismael ducked and ran from them all, feet pounding into the dirt; fleetingly, he saw his sisters, Rosie troubled as she had been, and Cristina both sorry and awakened; streets led into other streets, men and dogs that restlessly walked the earth at night taking refuge in the circles the lights made in the dark. The tangled weeds that lay outside town scratched Ismael's legs. He did not have time to turn his head to look for the man, and all that he heard was the way his chest shook and rattled up into his gorge. He turned into the dark of an abandoned cantina, far outside town and overgrown with crawling, greedy vines that he tore aside. Inside, accumulated dust entered the delicate pink of his flared nostrils and caught in his throat. He clawed into the depth of a shadowy corner like a bat, and roosted there for some minutes.

But the doorway filled with the man, and he crowded into Ismael, the sour, curdled smell of his power-craving, corrupted breath choking Ismael when only minutes earlier he had glimpsed the possibility of real pleasure for the first time. The gun had gone back into the man's pocket during his pursuit.

Ismael felt the weight of the gun he had been given by the cartel and had always carried since for protection, but never used or ever wanted to use. Now he felt he did not have a choice, and the belligerence that had entered him as he ran from the man quickly constricted into pure fury and hatred which surged easily into the gun. He brought it up. He had more bullets than his grandmother had. Abruptly, he was in the volatile centre of her story and her fervour, which had driven him to this place.

He pulled the trigger and bullet after bullet went into the carcass in front of him, puncturing and penetrating. The coarse skin splattered open to reveal the transparent jelly of the plasma and the ruby-red, pulpy stringiness beneath as the bullets burned instantly through all the slowly formed strata of flesh and out on the other side, eradicating all inclinations. Only then did Ismael see that the menacing disdain stayed on his face as the thread of life slid out of the man and his greasy body fell to the grimy floor in spreading, soaking red. The foul smell of seared meat muddied the air, and one chunky hand clenched into an impotent fist below the man's belly, spotted with rust brown. Yellowed teeth, glimmering with saliva, showed in the dead open mouth like dull topaz.

There was a moment of abandon, when what Ismael had just done eliminated everything else from the cosmos, and then the overwhelmingly pathetic delusion of that clenched fist entered Ismael and he started to shiver uncontrollably. He felt his heart shudder-jitter in his chest as it never had. The shaking brought up the contents of his stomach to join the blood and entrails on the floor.

He knew he had to squash everything else down in himself, and leave the cantina.

Ismael left the man there, in the warm, eggy odour of the very beginning of rotting, threw the gun into the depths of the matted weeds, and walked back to the village he had always lived in, as his grandfather had tried and failed to on the last night of his life.

It took Ismael all night, and the moon and the stars did not comfort him. Neither did the hot tears that came for the first time in his adult life.

An hour outside town, he passed the well his grand-fathers had dug. The stone walls of the well were ridged and dimpled like the surface of a brain and dotted with pebbled, flaked dandruff, like the moon. Ismael stopped to crane his neck and look into the hole, hoping for something to tell him what to do. The moon was there, in the white cres-cents on the water, glistening at the very bottom, thirty feet down, but it told him no more than it had from the sky that night.

Snakes rested where he could not see them in the sun-retaining crevices of the rock piles by the road, but he knew they were there. At times, his mind went back to the aban-doned cantina and the body stewing in its own disintegration.

No solace came to Ismael, except for the memory of the woman's aquamarine eyes and the hope that one day he would somehow be able to unlock them again.

Ismael recoiled from the vividly remembered snake eye which made him afraid.

When he arrived back at the village in the grey dew of the early morning, Jose, who knew everything that happened everywhere and what to do about it, told him that he had to go, somewhere that nobody would know him, and stay there. The dead man's friends would come looking and if they found Ismael in the village, everyone would be punished. Jose thought the dead man had been a bodyguard and foot soldier; the one with the snake eye was the true collaborator of the green-eyed woman.

He did not have time to see Rosie or Cristina before he went.

A new, persistent restlessness came into Ismael that would not leave again. It continued to swing strong, back and forth, up so high touching the eagles in the brazen blue sky, now dragging through the pebbly dirt low and close to the ground where the ants were and beneath that to the foment that had brought Ismael to the green-eyed woman, and it brought the poisonous scorpions out.

All else faded away. Ismael was alone, he would be alone; solely him and what lay inside and outside, with no illusion of a filter in between.

He ran onto the highway where he jumped into the rutted metal back of a red farm truck with an unfamiliar blue bordered Guerrero state licence plate. It was driven by an old man with a much longer body and a thinner, more aquiline face than anyone in the village or the area around it had.

Ismael used one finger pointed at himself, shaken and put to the ear to say,

—Me no hear, me no hear, and the same finger first pointed at himself and shaken and a Pac-Man hand shape held by his mouth, snapping up baddies, told the Guerrero man, Me no talk-talk, me no talk-talk.

He sat on top of the far right corner of the truck bed, bracing himself with his bone-tired arms. From the red farm truck he went to a small, pale blue beat-up sedan and then to a sixteen-wheeler before he finally got to the city. Exhaustion and confusion dragged him in and out of a state between sleep and wakefulness. His disorientation smelled like burnt flesh, and on its edges he sensed rather than saw a white Volkswagen with the hood painted blue.

Through these hours, an astringent weight started behind Ismael's eyes and slowly dripped down his trachea into his bowels.

Chapter Three

*O*range its veins show through, same butterfly its wing. Centre segment it pale. Towards edges, skin its orange become can see through. Me Rosie-old me bite into orange, taste sweet juice its, sweet spill tongue, sweet spill chin. Ismael-strong, brother mine away long time not know where. Orange it sweet, but me Rosie-old me see ugly brown scorpion it there on scrabbly dirt by bush. Not like, feel little scared. Now see scorpion make me think again Ismael-strong. Bad happen Ismael-strong me Rosie-old me know me always know since many year bad will happen. But hope no more hope no more. Have taste sweet spill there have there have. Me Rosie-old me need push bad out.

Me Rosie-old me sit top step. Eat orange sweet spill mouth. Cristina-big angry scorpion there, me Rosie-old me not tell. Me Rosie-old me better not tell. Secret that fine good calm calm me Rosie-old me push bad out.

Me Rosie-old me eat sweet spill orange.

Rosie went back into the house. It was the mute and

muted afternoon hours when she stood in front of the hammock loom.

On the dirt next to Rosie's left foot was the tiny, evil scorpion. Its blindly waving pincers cleared the way for its venomous tail, uplifted in righteousness. But the scorpion found itself in empty space. There was nothing in the air around Rosie that divided the human flesh from the rest; all widened into abstraction, pushing the scorpion off on its spiky way.

Rosie picked up a smooth, whitish pebble fanned with grey and rubbed her finger over the hard sureness of it. She went outside for a moment. Enough light penetrated the trees outside the house to make soft circles that waved back and forth on the ground.

The world was there. Everything in it was there. But no part of it could be packaged and handed over to Rosie neatly and with dull finality, nor even with dull questions. And she did not attempt to explain anything to anyone.

She stood in the sun and watched the thin spiked leaves of the palms reach over the rippled eye-shaped leaves of other trees. The only thing above her was blue and birds of prey with their wings spread full. Clouds dappled the bluish-grey ceiling of the world, and they drifted slowly. They echoed the motions of Rosie's thoughts and feelings. She could easily put those clouds and the exact way they moved into her hands, but she did not.

The things that the outside world boxed away under interpretations, reasons, rationalizations, motivations, explanations, analyses, conclusions, decisions, preferences, and more, did not figure in her.

There were only the clouds, and their inner echo.

After Ismael's desertion, Cristina claimed the axis of their shared world, chaining herself to it, for the moment plunging against it as futilely as a pig.

Ismael had been the man of the house. When he slapped Cristina's arid cheeks with his strong hands, he expected to extinguish the silly disturbances in her. It was his duty to tamp down the embers around her just before they caught fire. Now Ismael's patriarchal bluster was gone, and Rosie only looked away, so as not to see the threatening obscenity in her baby sister.

Cristina knew not ever to talk to anyone about what exactly might have passed to make Ismael leave. She had seen newspapers. *El cuerpo sin vida de la persona decapitada, mucho mucho malo.* They were always filled with news of the *chicos malos*; large photos of severed fingers making bloody spots on a pavement outside Acapulco, and heads ending in shiny strings of muscle and bone hanging from wood stakes on a beach. Close-ups of decapitated people, a motherly looking female with an open, wet cut from eye to mouth among the danger-seeking young men with bandanas over their dead foreheads.

Once she had copied the lines of the words *'¿Donde narcos?'* from the newspaper headline above some pictures onto a piece of paper just for the jeopardy thrill of being linked to those bloody photos. When the tailor Chabelo had seen the paper and saw the newspaper that the words had come from, he had ripped both up, burned the pieces to ashes, threw the ashes into the toilet pit and pissed and shat mightily on them, then told Cristina never to ask questions or write anything about the narcos ever again. They were all around, Chabelo said. Even to talk or write of them was dangerous. He had drawn a diagram, a circle with lines to other circles with more lines leading from them to more circles that filled the entire sheet of paper.

Ismael was gone, that was all.

Cristina moved her pink and green hammock from the small beige back room that she had always shared with Rosie into the larger turquoise front room in the house, where Ismael had slept. It was the first time she had ever slept in a room on her own.

And the first time she had ever been able to decide what to do with the money. Their cousins gave it to her for Rosie and herself, now that Ismael was gone. The first time she got it, Cristina went to the big store, but she fancied nothing. Not the cream in the middle of the chocolate buns, or the floury pink and white marshmallows smushed into a plastic bag. Salt didn't promise the same awakening tang that it always had for her.

She looked around. Herman who worked in the big store was in the back room with his two younger sons, watching football on television. They did not pay any attention to her. Cristina could not see Herman's wife, who sometimes minded the store. She walked over to the end of the front counter and the row of open tubs of cheap sweets and chewing gum. One hand rested on the counter as she stood close to it, and then it closed over a red sweet and went back into the long sleeve of her shirt and into the pocket of her yellow stretch shorts.

She walked out of the store and down the street, making a left by the Protestant church onto the back road that Ismael always told her to be careful walking on, because mean dogs lived on it; the road that she walked as often as she could now, longing for the dogs to bite her. They never did.

Past the big piece of land on the corner where they sometimes bought tomatoes when there were none ripe in their garden, and past the house of their cousin who had

44

albino patches on her dark skin. Next to it was the house with the cement porch that opened right onto the street, not like most houses which were set back from the street with enough packed dirt between house and street for people to sit out front looking at who walked by, for children to play, plants to be set out in old plastic buckets and cook-pots, animals to be roped up.

Cristina sat down on the neighbour's porch. Her cousin's completely albino youngest child came out into the sun a few houses away, her pale eyelashes blinking rapidly as the light hit her. Cristina picked the baby up and sat down again. The baby usually stayed in a playpen inside so she would not be exposed to the sun, and she sat docilely in Cristina's lap, not moving except for the fluttering pink eyelids and, behind them, the pale, watery eyes flickering fast back and forth like static on a television screen. It took her a long while to bring out her small, damp tongue to touch the sweet when Cristina put it into her hand. She licked it a few times, but for some minutes she did not taste it again. Cristina stroked the white hair that was combed and rubber-banded tightly into small pigtails from ear to ear, to make a princess's crown.

They sat until the stolen sweet went completely into the baby's mouth. Cristina carried her back into the dark house and put her into her pen where she sat still with her eyes closed in the middle of the silky shadows that caressed her.

Then Cristina went home and wondered what she could do now to slake her thirst, the thirst of the unnamed. The air pulled insistently on the flesh of her face. She felt the skin dry and tight on her forehead. It stretched thin over the red bumps on her cheek.

There was a baseball game that afternoon and Cristina sauntered along to it, the heart-shaped white plastic sunglasses that Spectacles had bought her on the bridge of her nose, sticky, candy-pink lipstick on her lips under the definite outlines of a dark, wine-red lip liner. She revelled in the feeling of her hips swaying satisfyingly in her tight zebra print skirt and in the awareness of the day lying hot and lazy in front of her, in a way she had never been able to when she knew Ismael was around with his watchful, censoring eyes. It was just her now, no Ismael. Rosie might as well not have been there.

Herman, who worked in the store, came up to bat. Jose the scorekeeper was sitting next to him and had been turning the zeroes of the village score into cats on his notepad, adding whiskers, an upside down triangle for the nose and two for ears, and dots for eyes.

Every time an inning ended and the village had not scored, the men drinking beer on the rocks beside the base-

46

ball field turned to Jose and held the fingers of both hands up to either side of their mouths to become whiskers. But Herman was a good batter, and everyone leant forward in anticipation. Sure enough bat came onto ball just right and it went off into the trees where nobody would find it again. Herman ran joyfully around all the bases and slid onto home plate.

The fingers and thumb of one of Jose's hands came together to become the ball and the index finger of the other hand became the bat as it swung round, smack into the ball. The hand that had been the ball became an open palm fading into the distance.

Even the things nobody could find, even the unknown, had a shape in your body.

But at that moment nothing in Cristina's body had a shape that she could detect. There was only an uneven sputtering.

She lifted her feet in their lavender rubber sandals and banged them hard against the bank of rocks she sat on alongside the other women, again and again; the bang stopped the murmur in the air that laid a miasma over Cristina. She remembered those times as a little girl, walking to school alongside her father, and the way bringing that stick down onto the rocks had done the same for her then.

47

But she was not a little girl any longer. Her father was dead.

Cristina knew what her father would have wanted her to do now, what he had expected Ismael to do. And her mother, who stood heavy breasted in the centre of every crowd, a rope tied around her flowered dress just at the swell of her large hips. Busily solving everyone's problems and making sure that the world went around as it should, when she wasn't industriously cleaning and cooking in her small lean-to. She had not left herself time for anything else, and she would have told Cristina not to either.

Her mother's questioning, drooping brown eyes over her long, flat nose came into Cristina's mind.

Her parents had thought always of Rosie; to make Rosie safe and protected, to keep all in its place around her so that she could feel where her own place was.

But Cristina also knew that her parents had seen her unrest and commotion. That was who she was. She and Rosie needed Ismael; and Ismael had fled after doing what nobody could ever have thought he would do.

Juan-Deafy stood behind home plate with his cart and his horn, a cooler at his feet.

Ismael had bought her and Rosie an occasional beer, but always he preached fervently and virtuously about those in the village who worked to drink, only to lie in the foetal position in their hammocks for hours on end, pools of urine and vomit spreading beneath them on the concrete floor.

Cristina felt the crowd's eyes pop outside of their sockets, swaying on stalks, following her as she walked to Juan-Deafy and got herself a cold beer. And then another, and another. She bought up all the beer Juan-Deafy had in the puddle of cold water at the bottom of his white foam ice chest. The alcohol washed through her body with her blood, entered her heart where it was fully welcomed, was circulated, was pushed out again.

A door came into view that Cristina could go through to somewhere else, even if it was just for a few hours. It opened and Cristina stepped out. The formless energies that had been rising all day were substantial, but everything drew in now and the rest was forgotten. Cristina laughed at the sensation of it. The laugh gurgled in her belly and swelled up, thrusting out the monsters clinging inside her and deadening the ashes.

Next to her on the rock, Neidi laughed with her; everything softened and blurred, and Cristina was happy. The carbonated yeast of the beer expanded beneath her and cushioned her. She did not need anything else.

Cristina pointed at Neidi, then turned her hand palm up, down, up again.

—You, what up? You, what do now?

She bobbed her head up and down to accompany the gestures.

Another good hitter was up at bat. Another run for the village, there was hope yet! The other team only had three runs on them – it could happen! You never knew.

Across from them, a man Cristina had never seen before leant against his red motor scooter, a tiger print kerchief knotted over his hair above his square face. He must have come with the other team. Behind the protection of her heart-shaped sunglasses, Cristina's eyes stayed on him; on the lump in the middle of his strong neck, on the white T-shirt that stretched tight across the muscles of his arms. On the motor scooter that could take him anywhere fast and easy, with room for only one other behind him, not like the clumsy trucks most men in the village had that were loaded with families, chairs, sacks of feed, mass and burden.

A year after Ismael married Flat-face, Cristina had married too. Antonio, large, laughing Antonio who could hear. Her parents and Ismael liked him, for his laughter sucked in Cristina's angst and dissolved it. He touched her for the first time behind the small health clinic after a fiesta. She remembered it from somewhere else.

They were all happy in their own worlds for what had felt like a long time; she with Antonio, Ismael with Flat-face, and Rosie with their parents. There had been a child in her womb too; it dropped out and onto the dirt when she fell off a ladder, but Cristina and Antonio knew another would grow in her.

One day, Cristina was walking to the big store to buy salt and passed the clinic; a coin fell out of her hand and rolled till finally it fell flat on its front behind the clinic, and when she went to pick it up, there on the back wall of the clinic like a broad slug was Antonio's familiar back, jerking against that girl Claudia.

And then his laughter did not heal any longer.

Cristina had no alternative but to try to empty out her emotions for him. She tried to suck it back into herself, to chew on it and then swallow it down like the cows did, but it became stuck in her entrails. She had no place to put it. It seeped through the tissue of her arteries and came back out through her skin, in odorous perspiration. She ground down as hard as possible onto the sinews, tendons, gristle, and fat of all the meat she could find. Her molars started breaking off; she needed to find something else.

The cows chewed; the owls spit up; what could she do?

Claudia, who had been with Antonio against the wall of the medical clinic, came to the house to see her, pinched her all over, and bit Cristina on the neck.

—I love you friend, she said before she laughed in Cristina's face and left.

Cristina could not sleep for a week.

Night after night, Cristina forcibly plunged Antonio into the same fight. He tried to resist her; but she was too strong for him. She was too strong for anyone in the village except her parents and Ismael. He turned his head away or nodded and kept on eating. The man whose every body marking Cristina knew became someone she could not recognize.

He spent less and less time in their house, and then one day he was gone, to live with Claudia, where he had stayed ever since.

Cristina moved back into the lean-to at the edge of town where her parents and Rosie lived; a month later, Ismael decided Flat-face would never have babies and came back to his sisters to build his new house onto the old one. And a month after that, their parents were gone.

They had always returned to each other, she, Ismael, and Rosie.

After Antonio, Cristina believed that she would live together with Ismael and Rosie until they died, her siblings always absorbing her unease in the way she now felt only they could.

One by one they would become old and shrivel away, and those that remained would not fill the absence with anything else, but live with the ghosts in exactly the same way. Rosie would die first, because she was the oldest; then Ismael, when he was very old, and finally she herself.

Cristina still admired the strong, brown forearms of the men, some with a flicker of golden hair. It estranged her pleasurably from her worries; but now she told herself firmly that was where it stopped. Unlike with other things in her life, she obeyed her own command on this.

The men in the village had known her all of her life, and they knew Antonio and Ismael. None of them approached her for they knew that Ismael would come down on them powerfully.

Once when she rode to the big city with Ismael, a glue sniffer had taken a DVD out from under his shirt and shown it to her. Ismael was walking in front of her and did not see. There was a hairy, contracting crimson on the cover of the DVD, taking in a male back curved like a bow. The glue sniffer saw her look away quickly, and the kamikaze satisfaction oozed out of him like the glue from his bottle. Cristina had startled; it was the first glance in a long time of that other, secret world of sweaty bodies coming together and knowing each other in that ardent, gentle, consuming way. She had forgotten that many other people were rooted by this world, that it constituted the main part of their lives. The reminder tore at the life that she had constructed with

Ismael and Rosie and the sky was flat and harsh above her for a time.

Then one day, warm air wafted over her in a leisurely way as she lay in the hammock hung outside the house; and here a cooler gust dawdled over her arm. Weed heads tumbled like precious jewels through the air. Cristina stared through the woven palm fronds of the roof at the uttermost blue above. Everything was liveable again, and again she remembered why she did not want the world of flesh any longer, and why she lived with her brother and sister.

But it was a triangle, the three of them: Ismael anchoring, Rosie pacifying, she motoring forward. It didn't work with only two. Cristina had to figure out another way to live.

For now, her answer was the man on the red motor scooter. The scooter was parked beneath the trees at the end of the baseball field, and he sat with his back against the rough striped trunk of a palm tree.

Still floating on the cloud of the beer but feeling the air beginning to hiss slowly out underneath her, and with the knowledge that there was no more beer in Juan-Deafy's cooler, Cristina again got to her feet and promenaded in front of the crowd, which was restless to be entertained. There had been no real gossip since Ismael's disappearance three months before. It had been the most nefarious, surprising scandal for years and it was still affecting the day-to-day life of the village, which was reforming itself around the hole where Ismael once stood. He and Jose were consulted on all the things that the others did not immediately see how to handle. Ismael's discretion held the secrets of many and he had guided them through the time of the narcos. He was unquestionably the most esteemed deaf man in town.

But even his departure was eventually digested. They knew that there was a fist fight between Ismael and an unfamiliar man at the fiesta and that both of them had disappeared into the dark, but their Ismael would never have left his sisters for anything. In all the village, only Jose knew that the other man had later been found dead in the old cantina by his people.

Most of the village thought Ismael must have rejoined the narcos or been killed by them and buried deep in the ground in some secret, dank jungle. Some thought he had a woman in the city, maybe a bad woman.

A few old men in front of the biggest store in town still gnawed it over, tearing the last threads of flesh and speculation from it and smacking their lips, but for the rest of the village, only the bones of the thing were left. Ismael had disappeared, leaving Cristina and Rosie on their own.

Estevanya, always good for filth around her house and

in her self, had gone permanently clean. A visiting schoolmaster now came every Saturday to see Estevanya. The schoolmaster sat at the plastic Corona table, staring at Estevanya's coffee-coloured eyes, *'Bonita muy muy bonita cexi linda! Guapa caliente mami, mi mamita, mamita Hermosa . . .'*

He was Mexican and not Maya, from Nayarit where there were orange groves and an island full of Asian Mexicans named Chung. He did not even drink, and when the schoolmaster was not staring at her eyes, he sat with Estevanya outside her now tidy house and yard, playing with Estevanya's children.

So when Cristina, newly left alone by her brother and seen drinking for the first time that anyone could remember, fixed her eyes on the man with the red motor scooter, the man that Estevanya had told Ardrogna was sucking the remnants of last night deeper into his nose and looking with chemical-tasting, dry, slack mouth at the teenage girls in their short neon skirts, the crowd was delighted.

They were even more satiated when she wobbled straight to him, occasionally stumbling, her body going outside of its lines. The hot sun and the beer insulated her. She was intoxicated further by the activity of her body and its effect on the world – the dust her feet kicked up, the weight of her gold earrings pulling lightly on her earlobes with each step she took.

The vigour was beautiful and alive in her eyes as she looked only at him, but nobody saw it. They only saw clumsiness.

Here he stood for her, strutting in his boots, baseball cap pulled low over the eyes. His eyes had a snigger in them that flared up whenever he thrust people into the quick snapping snare of his judgements, which was often, but his orange Oakley sunglasses hid his eyes from Cristina.

Suddenly Cristina's ravening became great. She saw only the square, white teeth when he smiled at her, and the nod of his head when she pointed at herself and then reached out into the air in front of her, twisted one hand, and then pointed at him to ask if she could ride behind him on the red scooter. The gestures grounded her again, made her remember where she was.

Cristina felt again that her body was unquestionably there. It was as there as the eagles perched on the very top branches of the nude trees at the edge of the baseball field, stoic, blinking kings inspecting the damaged realm. All that she felt, all of the unsteady fretfulness and oases of calm, was still in her body and would always be. And all that she said through her body carried all of her self with it, in its vulnerability and truth. She did not know if other people were the same way, but she knew that when she watched the speaking people talking to one another, she felt differently than when she watched them use her language.

When she climbed behind the man with the tiger kerchief on the scooter and wrapped her arms around him, she trusted that he was there too. She had forgotten the certainty of a wide, soft, alive back. She felt the most protected she had since Ismael left.

He started the scooter and they rode past the animated crowd. Cristina closed her eyes. An unsteady shining coloured the back of her eyelids. It balanced into a sequinned expanse that shimmered as brilliantly as the sun on the ocean Cristina saw on television. It swathed her into a liquid, beating song of which there was no inside, no outside; an entirety of warm, damp rose and into it disappeared all that ailed her.

She opened her eyes just in time to see her house go by. Through the open door, she saw Rosie sitting watching television, those familiar scrawny calves and puffy feet in their torn black rubber sandals stretched out in front of her. Momentarily, Cristina felt that was where she should be, next to her sister in the cool, calm shade, but then she closed her eyes again and pressed her arms tighter around the man's chest. Today she could fly.

Chapter Four

In the big city, Ismael laid concrete all day in the hot sun. When the wilting dusk came, he followed the other men to the store closest to wherever they were working, where they each bought a bottle of beer with the day's wages. Always, Ismael was tempted to buy another and then another, as the other men did, but he remembered his admonishments to his sisters about drinking.

The old delineations of Ismael's life had lifted off the ground, the new lines had not been completely drawn just yet, and space was left for the divine. He did not want that space to be filled with the confusion that alcohol brought.

After he finished his one beer with the other men, he began the long walk up the mountains above the city. Past the tourist restaurants with cartoon characters above the doors, past the electronic repair shops with their metal shelves full of inexplicable hanging wires, gears, and gadgets covered in dust; past the houses of the remote, judicious, upstanding, chattering citizens with their iron gates and driveways. Past even the open-faced rooms built one on top of another where many of the men he worked with lived. He waved to their wives cooking together on grills over foil pans on the terraces outside the rooms.

Ismael followed the same road as it snaked up and up the side of the mountain. The tan of the road rose and fell, dust distorting his vision as his feet kicked it up to float in the air. The one-room lean-tos balanced on stilts on either side gave way to a long stretch of desiccated, brown, twisted undergrowth. After that, just before the very top of the mountain, under the cool breadth of a brawny, spreading tree, were steps carved plumb into the narrow chest of the peak. And up these steps were the four upright boughs and palm frond roof that Ismael now called home. His red hammock swayed in the breezes. Plastic bags hung from the fork on top of one of the posts and in them were a bottle of water, soap, a towel and washrag, a roll of toilet paper, a can of spray-on musk deodorant, his clothes, powdered laundry soap, a comb, and his toothbrush and toothpaste.

Beneath him was the velvety green of the jungle roof. Smoke clouded from a fire in the distance, and he could not see any of the buildings of the city or any other signs of human existence. It was easy to forget that anyone else had emotions. Ismael did not forget his own.

He sank onto the hammock. This moment was when

Ismael stepped off the tightrope that by day took him over the chaos that the seducing dark brought to him.

All day long, Ismael watched the men he worked with push away superstitions from themselves with the structure of words, much as he had been able to back at home.

He cried again when he set up this hammock on the top of the world, freeing some of the disquiet that had loitered since he killed the man. It had been a relief, but much stayed in him and it was strong.

Once he was alone, the acid that he swallowed down in the daytime came back up into Ismael's throat. His frustration broke loose from the flimsy apparatuses he had been able to develop to channel it since getting to the city.

It was all still so new to him. He was trying to understand how to moor this self who had killed, and without being able to communicate fully with anyone. He felt he was floundering in a bottomless, hostile ocean. He tried to go numb, but he did not know how to do that either. He only pretended to the other men that he knew how.

Where had his grandmother Alondra gone after shooting his grandfather? How had she lived? If Ismael knew, he would never have shot the man. Nothing unresolved would have stayed in his arteries and her story would not have held such power for him. The charged potential was there in his sisters too, and he was now certain that it would blast through both of them in some way or other. He pictured Rosie, impassive and careful, and Cristina, hungry and struggling. How were they? Did they understand that the situation was permanent, as Ismael was sure it was, and that it was latent in them too? Were they angry with him?

As he lay in the red hammock, Ismael talked to himself with his hands, gathering the shattered pieces that lay inside of him back together into a solid whole. He told himself who he was; where his home village lay. He described the beauty of the jungle in front of his eyes, and his position there in the hammock on the mountain up above it. Then he knew where he was again and he felt inside his self again.

It took several hours for the unruliness to subside, and for the face of the woman that had spurred him to kill to imbue the surface of his mind. Ismael remembered the aquamarine eyes that had become mirrors to him and released his soul, and wondered if he could unlock them again. The precious memory of that metamorphosis had been the only thing that could feed him for the first month he was in the city, and he took it out again and again till it became threadbare.

When the stuff of the memory was more hole than substance, with only the green of these glowing eyes remaining, Ismael started to speculate about the identity of the woman, and of the man he had killed. He was sure that it had something to do with the narcos, and Jose had thought so too, but he knew the woman was not married and did not have a lover, for he had asked surreptitiously the first time he had seen her. Was it her brother that he had shot? A cousin? What was their exact relationship and why had it meant so much? Was her life different now, after that night? Did she think of him?

The first time he had seen her, Ismael had been certain that it did not matter what the conditions of her life were, that she was separate from them. He was not so sure any more.

If it was the narcos, Ismael knew they would find him. They knew everything and were everywhere. They paid off children and old people as well as the men. In the city he would be found on his own, and the people around him would not be drawn into his punishment. And they might not kill him.

Here and now, as the darkness and the rootless melancholy gradually surrounded Ismael on his red hammock far up the mountain and distant from all that he had known – isolated even from the very tool with which he and most human beings give clarity to their lives – he spun wildly with the days and with sensations, and he wished in his whole body to know why he was in this place.

Just when he thought that he could not bear it any longer, he always fell asleep.

In the mornings, as the sun painted the sky a delicate, ephemeral pink and orange, Ismael woke to a laughing wind that swept his hair up and back and washed his face of the knowledge of what had gone and what lurked at the centre of the day, under his feet.

The precious illumination settled gently into the lining of his core. It was something he had never experienced in the village and something that he would not be able to explain in any language. By its very nature, it could not be put into stagnant words, and it was not completely of the body either.

When he felt it, one part of Ismael was glad that everything had happened to bring him here and experience the holy.

But then he swung out of the hammock and his feet touched the dehydrated ground again, and he walked laboriously down the precipitous steps on legs made unsteady by lack of sleep and a psychic disorientation.

Down the road, past the first few bends and curves, and he was at the wooden counter covered with bright pink flowered oilcloth. Ismael's dark, bemused eyes smiled as the bent, pear-shaped old woman behind the counter pointed to the jar of Nescafé. As she spooned it into his favourite

64

Te Amo mug with blue hearts on it, added three heaped spoonfuls of sugar, and put the pan of water onto the fire, Ismael lowered himself onto a stool facing her.

Pulling his blue Nike baseball cap lower over his eyes, he took the plate of unfamiliar chilaquiles. He thought of them at home; Rosie would be raking the powdery dust of the courtyard now, leaving a neat geometrical pattern of diagonal lines, and Cristina would be out back washing the breakfast dishes in soapy blue-grey water from the purple rubber bowl. Cristiano, the earnest boy from next door, and his little sister Lourdes, her round pot belly sticking out below her mauve T-shirt, would patter through the silt to inspect where the new day had taken the sisters.

He sipped the coffee and again he thought of the green-eyed woman. In the clear light of the day, Ismael was able to drown the thought in food. It fluttered and fought for its life for a few minutes, like an insect, but finally it gave up and died. Come the night, it would be resurrected.

He dabbed the last of the chilaquile juices off his plate with a piece of tortilla and got to his feet.

Down the road, down all the way to the bottom, bracing himself with his heels, and from there onto the main road. He raised his hand to all he came across, but nobody returned the gesture.

A white Volkswagen car with the engine hood painted

a dull blue sprayed stones as it cut in front of him, blocking the road. On either side were thorny bushes. In one glance, Ismael saw that the driver had a shaved head and a dirty white T-shirt rolled up above his bare pregnant-woman belly.

It was inevitable, and it became even more certain when Ismael saw a large, tattered photo taped onto the back of the lowered sun visor on the passenger side. Those green eyes he saw in his sleep, the eyes that writhed through his veins, finding their way to his crux, poking their way out of all the crevices and cracks of his self – these eyes looked back at him from the photo. She looked straight at the camera and her eyes took in all of the aching in Ismael.

But he could not look at her as long as he wanted to, because a fat, grasping hand was tearing at his throat and twisting far to the right. His skin pleated tightly and hotly as it was caught up and let go into a sharp burn. The flesh throbbed and glowed long after it was released.

The man's mouth opened forcefully, and it was as raw and hurt as the animals' pink cocks when they came out.

Then he got back into his car and sped off, the dust gaily riding the air behind the car before it returned to the ground. Ismael watched him go, and understood less about anything and had even less to hold onto than he had when lowering himself into his hammock the night before.

He did understand that they would take their retribution as and when they wanted, in pieces big and small.

He kept his eyes hard and fast on the ground now as he walked to work; and after a wave of greeting to the men he worked with, all of their faces blurring now into the man in the car, he kept his weary eyes on the wet grey cement and did not lift them.

The sun pressed its hand down on the gap between his trousers and his shirt, which had ridden up. It pressed so hard that Ismael thought he might tumble over and lie with the ants swarming on the cracked dirt. They would assemble in his ear holes and nostrils, and he would be still as they began to march around his eye sockets. After they worked at him a while, the vultures would come, and it would all be over.

The world faded to the hot sun on that band of flesh and to the cement he was laying, and it was a reprieve.

But the boss came shambling down to look at Ismael's work, as he rarely did; and Ismael had to look into his face. The mouth contorted, damp, brown lips pushing up first one cheek and then the other into a wrinkled, astonished grimace, sagging down for his enlarged red tongue to flap out and then for lips and tongue to be sucked back so far inwards that he looked like a toothless, bulgy-eyed old person.

Ismael had no idea what it meant or was supposed to mean, and today he had no emotional reserves to draw on to try to decipher it.

He looked unblinkingly into the face, nodded as if he knew just what was being talked about, and got back to work. Sludge wrenched on his sandals as he shouldered past grimacing faces.

But again the boss came, and Ismael did not know what else to do but to repeat the hated gestures he felt he made a thousand times a day here, the motions he had never, ever needed to make at home.

—Me no hear, me no talk.

The boss had written something on paper, but Ismael could not read or write more than a very few words, and none of the jittery black lines on the paper shaped themselves into anything that meant something to him. They were twisting, restless worms, that was all, far removed from him and everyone else. He shook his finger, pointed at the paper, repeated the gesture and then pointed at his ear.

—Me no read, me no hear.

With an angry look in his small eyes, the lids pushed together by fat, the boss glared at Ismael.

Eventually, the texture of time on Ismael's skin and the glue of heat and monotony began to fill some of the fissures.

But as the day went on and the sun grew blistering, the

man with the pink birthmark over his chin who always worked next to Ismael tried to speak to him, then the woman in the shop Ismael walked to on his break, to buy a bag of Doritos. He did not see anything correlating to what they were trying to say in their eyes. He felt his nods of feigned comprehension become less and less believable, to himself and to everyone else. Finally, when the man next to him, adamant about something, loomed over Ismael again, he felt the tail end of his spirit leave and squirm fast to tunnel into the dirt. He could not nod or pretend any more. He saw malice all around him, in every raised brow and curl of the lip; every utterance was a jeering, rattling curse. The looming questions of the man in the car, the man he had killed, the mysterious green-eyed woman, his inability to understand, and all that he understood far too well wove together into a web, and Ismael felt himself a fly stuck fast in it. The more he struggled, the more the web closed onto him.

He turned his back on the cement block wall he had been working on and walked off through the sand and onto the tarmac of the road. Tomorrow he would have to find another job; but it scarcely mattered to him. The days melted into each other in this strange place and one reason to do something was as good as another. Ismael only knew that he could not let himself start drinking, that he had to work at something, depend on himself, and stay as far away from the perilous ambiguity of other people as possible.

He thought of the village, of how people there used their steady hands to make the curved shape of the edge of the world, an edge that was weighty. Then they held the other hand under the hand that was the sky and said, Out there is near the edge. But now you are here.

The edge had always been there, somewhere else. Here was the village. Ismael had known that and lived by it; but it was not until now that he felt the edge. It was something real, and he was lurching on it. Any minute, he could fall off and be gone.

He thought of Rosie and Cristina, and Ismael understood how living felt for each of them better than he ever had.

He turned towards the centre of town, to fortify himself with tacos and a Coca-Cola before the long walk up to his hammock and before the feathery dark came to sweep at him with sharp claws again.

Chapter Five

Not know where Cristina-big. Cristina-big gone two days since with man on red scooter. Ismael-strong gone more longer. Me Rosie-old me OK fine OK fine. Cristina-big and Ismael-strong will fine OK too. Important remember big strong tree, important keep big strong tree there in mind. No spiky tree no spiky tree keep spiky tree far away better.

Rosie was alone in the jungle, in one of the clearings where people had cut firewood over the years. A splintery branch, taller and wider than Ismael, had separated from the main trunk of a tree and become tangled with the tops of other trees. The smaller limbs curled together to hold up the branch, but this safety net could let go at any time.

A bug bit her and her ankle prickled suddenly with pain. She felt downwards to try and brush it off.

Under the hanging wood, pig and cow bones lay on the leaves. Patterns grew on the bones as they rested in the jungle, freed now from the flesh they had once supported.

Brown fluffed into moss-green stain, and white spread on top.

Rosie looked at the bones for a long time. She held them and was reassured by them. Then she sat down on a log behind the trees, bent forward and peeled the bark off some twigs, removing the soft outer protection and leaving only the white heart of the branch. No sun reached her now, not even dim patterns of shadow and light.

But the other branch still hung above her head and she knew it was there.

Rosie went back to the house. It had rained the day before and shallow pools of standing water covered the way at some points. An empty plastic Coca-Cola bottle was on the sand of the path, and the children kicked it along for a while, until they accidentally kicked it too high and a snarl of grasses and twigs caught it fast. There were many other bottles on the path or lying in the ditches on either side of it next to the shiny foil of sweet and salt wrappers.

She allowed herself to glide on top of the thick heat as she walked. She did not look at any of the people she passed. Ardrogna the village gossip, with her square, manly face surrounded by tightly slicked back hair and her broad nose, was sitting in front of her house. She leapt up as Rosie approached, planted herself in front of Rosie on the path, and demanded,

—Cristina-big since gone two days! With big man kerchief tiger, two-fingers astride scooter, zoom off fast. Me see she wobble-wobble away with him! You think she OK? Gone forever or back next few days? What you do, now you alone? You never alone before your life! But now parents gone, Ismael-strong gone, Cristina-big gone!

Other heads peered over Ardrogna's shoulders, and Rosie saw other faces become greedy for details. They were animals running for food pitched on the ground. They scrambled for a crust to push into their hungry mouths, to tide them over till the next day.

Rosie handed over minute details of her days alone when they demanded them. She told them that she knew Cristina was all right and would be back.

—Cristina-big, she palm-down palm-down stay here far past into present here body. Now Ismael-strong gone, she confuse. All move round chest, all move round mind. She away flat-palm over there, somewhere. Upright palm ahead of self, some day not too far in future she back. Me palm-on-chest – me feel, me know she will back. Me calm, me OK.

Some people kept jumping at her throat, claiming more of the account and of her. She threw them morsels until finally they were satisfied and went away. They would regurgitate what she had told them to other people, like inelegant owls feeding their young.

This time, Rosie did not see the scorpion; she was too distracted by Ardrogna. It darted from one pungent foot to the next, coming close to each. The claws came within a millimetre of Ardrogna's puffy, square foot, which trembled enticingly with each arrogant utterance, but just as the stinger came down to strike, the foot fell quiet.

Appendage curling back into position, the scorpion scuttled off.

Neidi and Juan-Deafy were sitting on plastic chairs outside the store opposite the house with the blue drawing of a cow on it. Seeing Ardrogna's assault on Rosie, they looked at each other with doubt. The village knew Rosie had always drawn straight paths for herself through the parameters of her life. Hammock to outhouse. Outhouse to kitchen. Kitchen to yard. Yard to store and tortilleria. Tortilleria to house. On Sunday, house to church and then back. Variations from these paths were occasional and made only when necessary. She made steady and measured progress to the places she needed to go. Probably that was enough to sustain her through the absences of Ismael and Cristina, Neidi and Juan-Deafy told each other with their eyes. Foolish Ardrogna, they told each other in the same way. Words made Rosie into something else. For now, they would keep watching her, and so would everyone else in the village; and not all of them were like Ardrogna and her kind.

Rosie continued on her way. Up to the sky she looked, up to the gleaming blue she loved and the birds that knew how to stay buoyant atop thin air. And finally Rosie looked to the ground again, for she could not look up any longer.

Back at the house, she crouched over the fire as she boiled water for her favourite chicken flavoured instant noodles; she searched out the sweet peas and squares of salty carrot in the soup and slurped down the thin noodles. After every morsel of food was gone, she held the bowl to her mouth and drank the savoury liquid down.

Me Rosie-old me love eat, eat. In mind there and chest there all move. Better ignore. Focus grease oily spill mouth down stomach. Food move down throat yum yum stomach it good me Rosie-old me like much. Smack smack taste good. Better ignore all else.

The thoughts that had filled her mind and the emotions that had filled her body unfastened, temporarily but for long enough.

She went to the outhouse to clean off the sweat of the long, hot day, and stepped into the half-inch of grey water underfoot, sticky and dirty with what feet and bodies brought in. The night was not cold so she did not heat the water, but poured it on straight from the metal pail in the light of a candle stuck onto the back of the toilet, watching as her shadow followed her on the cement block wall and the peeling paint of the metal door.

The shadow reached across the ceiling, and in that tiny room it was larger and more physical than the fragile Rosie trying to bathe. Tonight it pranced freely, but Rosie knew its leash could easily shorten.

In her white nightshirt, she wrapped herself tightly in a blanket in her hammock. On the television a girl with bright white teeth like Rosie had never seen before, black hair combed high and back, and pink blusher on her smooth cheeks ran screaming from a moustached man on a white horse.

Rosie watched the television flicker every night as her grandparents had watched the fire waver; and she was soothed into a dreamless, complete sleep in the same way they had been.

Cristina still felt the security of the man's back and the near revelation of the wind on her skin as they moved faster than she had ever moved in her life. But now her large, unwieldy bottom tingled from all the bumps it had ridden over in those two days, and the metal of the seat poked her from under the rubber matting. The man had not asked her once if she was all right.

At times, she thought yearningly of Rosie, of the impenetrable comfort that being by her side meant. But often enough, she remembered the two nights she had passed together with the tiger kerchief man in the man's one-room hut in a nearby village, and the desirous infatuation made her forget. When she imagined what Ismael would say if he knew where she was, her thin lips curved into a satisfied smile.

Her white plastic heart-shaped sunglasses were clipped into the front of her skirt, and every time they stopped, Cristina put them on and felt herself to be another woman; a woman like the ones she saw on television.

She saw more clearly than ever before what a different kind of life would have been like for her. Sometimes she went as far as to wish that she had been born into another world and to wonder if she would have been able to keep ahold of herself better in this other, formless existence. But then she squinted her eyes against the air coming fast at her over the man's shoulder, and everything else left her mind.

They stopped often at houses on the edge of towns, and the man motioned to Cristina to stay outside, under the shade of overhanging roofs and trees. He opened the seat of the scooter and took out a wrapped package that he carried into the houses, or else he brought packages out of the houses. Once, another man whose flab was held rigid by his shoulders came outside. When he turned to Cristina, a coloured lens in one eye made the iris into a snake's yellow and green slit. The oblong shape of a gun was there beneath the glittery belt of his jeans. Cristina felt she had seen that snake eye before, and when she searched through the rubbish at the sides of her crowded mind, she remembered.

At the fiesta they had all gone to together on Ismael's last night with them, that frighteningly inhuman eye had glinted out from the face of the man next to the woman she knew was somehow the reason that Ismael had left them. Ismael had not known Cristina watched him all of that night; that she had seen the new expression in his eyes when he looked at that green-eyed woman, as beautiful and elusive as a butterfly.

Cristina could smell it in the air, a surreptitious, brackish tang of underhand dealings and lust. She longed to follow it down, to root out the furtive intentions and get closer to wherever Ismael was. But these newspaper headlines and the numb eyes and slack mouths of the mutilated drug traffickers stayed with her, and she knew Ismael would have wanted her to forget about that part of it and put everything into Rosie.

Before she had time to separate each strand of her confused thoughts and lay them out where she could see them clearly, they were away from the house and the scorpion tattooed man, humming along on the scooter under playful trees that reached under trunks and back up towards the sky to form wooden curlicues.

But after seeing the man tattooed with scorpions, Cristina began to think more of Rosie and the village.

At the next stop, Cristina was invited inside for the first time. There were no packages at this stop – just a tender, dignified, almost emaciated but still graceful elderly man in his hammock in a cluttered, dirty house, who raised a hand to Cristina and met her eyes full on. He asked with a circled hand lifted to his mouth if she wanted some water; then moving a finger over his throat and four fingers of the other hand held on top of the nose and flapping downwards, like the slimy diagonal of a pig's snout, he told her that he was about to butcher the hog that lunged on its four stubby legs from its chain in the wood pen behind the house, two tusks of whitish-pink tissue wobbling from under its jaw. When Cristina turned to look at the hog, it strained lustfully on its chain, fleshy tusks shaking vigorously, but it was stuck. Cristina suddenly felt what it felt. The feeling was persistent and caustic. Her unnamed anxiety coiled anew inside her like snakes. She looked up above the hog's pen to see wings flapping frenziedly on top of other wings, moth-eaten feathers falling to the ground, beady eyes above sharp, pecking beaks drawing crimson, an eagle grasping insatiably onto a small, tender brown bird as it squawked its death rattle.

Neither of the men saw; they looked at the ground.

Soon, there were damp red curves beneath Cristina's fingernails where she chewed them down.

The older man began to speak to the scooter man, and Cristina wandered around the house. There was a framed photo near the ceiling of a big-eyed baby girl with a pink bow in her hair, grinning toothlessly for the camera. And underneath the photo, on top of a small wooden cabinet with Bambi painted on it in white, was a wind-up dog, the size of one of Cristina's short fingers, with outstretched paws, googly eyes, and a red tongue peeping out from its plastic face. She grabbed it and put it in her pocket just as, out of the corner of her eye, she saw the men looking her way.

Back on the scooter, Cristina fiddled with the toy dog, twisting the white plastic knob that protruded above its left haunch, making it flip ludicrously back on its hind legs. Touching the dog felt good in the same way that tonguing the broken teeth at the back of her jaw did; she worried at both until the remorse for deserting Rosie left her.

This time the air rushing past them did not transport her in the same way. When they got back to the man's house for the night, Cristina did not want to be with him. She felt that something gnawed with yellowed rodent teeth at the partitions of her self, the holes joined up into lace-work.

He was angry, and his calloused hand came down on her again and again. But it was not too bad. The red marks faded away in minutes, and he had not broken the skin anywhere on her. He took her straight away over the macadam of the highway, onto the pebbled side roads that gave way to hard, packed, red dirt; and then they were riding through the peaceful cornfields.

The mass of the corn rested its weight on the small road, making it even slighter. The light that burrowed deep into the corn was moulded into slivers and splinters determined enough to find their way out to hover on top of Cristina, the tiger-kerchief man, and the scooter as they rode along the road. Looking ahead, you saw only corn. Looking below, there was dust; looking above, there was heat.

Cristina felt the holes inside her knitting together again. This time, when she got home, she would make sure she was unchangeably cushioned no matter what came into her, and she would stay floating. Again she fingered the plastic dog and knew that it was real and constant. The dog rolled acquiescingly onto its back in her pocket, and she clenched it tight into her fist, as her mother had gripped the rosary where she stored those sanctifying, ghostly words from the priest's mouth. Cristina had only solidity in place of that, but solidity can be everything.

Cristina did have everything in those short minutes, as

they passed the green sign with the white lines that she did not understand but that she knew meant that she was almost to her village, where Rosie was and where she could feel the physical traces of Ismael. He was there in the dried brush-strokes in the paint on the walls of the house; his clothes were still folded and stacked in the tiny back room, and his tools were leaning against the back wall of the outhouse.

As they neared the village, the man sped up and the scooter went so fast that Cristina was blown clean. She squeezed her eyes shut, and at the same time she felt her sunglasses fall out of her skirt. She reached a hand down to rescue them, but the white plastic heart-shaped frames were gone, buried deep in the cornfields, along with the trans-formation they had offered.

She reached in front of the man and directed him through the streets to her house. The last of the children were out playing, not wanting to go home until they had to. They had chosen piles of dirt that were nearly all shadow to hide themselves away on. Only a movement you were not sure you had really seen told of the child, like a small modification at the bottom of a rock pool that made you realize there was a crab down there. At the sight of Cristina behind the man on the scooter, they ran inside to tell their mothers that she was back, and biting, bright eyes scurried from the houses to look at them flying past. Ardrogna ran in front of the scooter to spray Cristina with questions. The speed of the bike meant that Cristina could not answer any of them. But what Cristina understood of the questions in those instants before they were past Ardrogna on the road cut her to the quick.

—Cristina-big, Cristina-big! Me much happy you back! Rosie-old, she alone, she alone, she not talk no one since almost three days! Me see Rosie-old sad, big big sad. She never alone before her life. Now parents dead, Ismael-strong gone, you gone. My heart break, Rosie-old alone, you all leave her. But now you back. What happen with tiger kerchief man! What happen! What happen!

The scooter stopped in front of the stone house she pointed the man to with one hand, putting palm down in a sharp motion. As soon as she heaved her leg over the side of the scooter and her bottom, released from the buttress of the scooter seat, plopped into the air, he was gone.

Inside the house, Rosie sat on the red rubber chair next to the door, thin, squashy legs placed square on the cement floor. She barely looked up at Cristina as she entered the room. And when Cristina flapped her arm to get Rosie's attention, there was no change in the impassivity in Rosie's eyes. She slowly turned her head back to the wall and put one hand over the other in the clasp they knew well, those short fingers of Rosie's that moved slowly and carefully.

After Cristina made a special dinner of black bean empanadas with fresh, garlicky red salsa, Rosie offered up Coca-Cola in the big bottle she had bought at midday, even if it was warm and the bubbles were flattened by now. After dinner, Rosie set a pot of water over the fire and then put it in the outhouse for Cristina to wash with, although the day was warm and they would ordinarily have washed with cold water. After Cristina had bathed, Rosie beckoned to Cristina to come to sit between her legs on the front steps under the small section of corrugated tin roofing that extended over the front door. She searched Cristina's hair and pulled out any white hairs she found growing kinkily among the smooth black ones.

—Man not want old woman, Rosie told Cristina.

—Me pull out white hair, one day you have good man, Cristina-big.

The bottom line of their thighs sagged in the same way, one on the step above the other.

The bus bound for the big city went by, and its headlights passed slowly over each of the sisters. The light was a thick, finely hued stupor like sea glass, and it shone down on them and illuminated both Rosie and Cristina from inside out. Above them hung the bare pearl of the moon.

When the hammocks were rearranged and put up for

the night, Rosie moved Cristina's hammock back into the room they had shared, the small beige room with the swathe of salmon paint on one wall and the pink and red butterfly they had painted by the door in nail varnish as little girls; the room they had been born in and where Cristina now impulsively, intensely hoped they would both die. Maybe even Ismael would die here.

She remembered the snake-eyed man and the identical cruelty in both of his eyes. He and his friends would be after Ismael, and perhaps after her and Rosie too. He had left her alone for now, but that was no guarantee. They would make sure they always knew where Ismael's sisters were. Maybe none of the siblings would die of old age in their parents' house. Still, she hoped.

Cristina could not contemplate escaping somewhere else. They would find her anywhere and everywhere in the small radius she considered going. Ismael, she thought, must be much further out. Maybe he was eating fish by the ocean she had always dreamed of seeing.

Added on top of that, there was no way Rosie would leave the village for longer than a trip to the market, and especially after the guilt that had come to her after what Ardrogna said, Cristina would not leave her sister again. The sisters would stay in the village and wait for whatever came. The cruellest possibilities would be for Ismael. She hoped that whatever happened to her and Rosie, it would not be too painful.

Cristina knew with certainty that whatever had started on the night of the fiesta was still alive and was nowhere near its end; that no matter how good she was, no matter how close to Rosie she stayed, none of them would be able to get away from it. The spreading vibrations were recoiling.

Tonight, the sisters' two hammocks were strung from the same hook, and they swung side by side whilst their favourite telenovela played on the television. Quickly, Rosie told Cristina what had happened in the show in the time she had been away. Last night the good-looking young man had found out that the girl with big breasts and the very short red skirt had been lying to him when she told him that they had to work together. He had to apologize to his beautiful girlfriend tonight, but who knew if she would accept the apology? She was the rich one. He had always been lucky to have her anyway.

Rosie and Cristina did not understand what was being said, but they watched this show every night. They understood people falling in and out of love, people going behind each other's backs, people stealing or planning secretly in dark corners, people dying. What more was there?

After Rosie fell into potent, transparent sleep, the knees of her skinny legs drawn up against her full body and her small hands pillowing her head with its round of long, thin black hair, Cristina stared at the ceiling. At this time the previous night she had been with the tiger-kerchief man.

The proof that all of it had happened, existed in actuality, and not just in her festering, promiscuous mind was the plastic wind-up dog that still lay in her pocket. She would keep it as a reminder; and she would remember also what had made her come back, and the splendour of the light that had come down on her when she was back in her house in the village with Rosie.

Finally, Cristina fell asleep; and her sleep too was potent and transparent, as it had not been in the nights away from the village.

For the next few weeks, Cristina did not slurp up bottlefuls of words to suck on till they went dry and acrid. She let them slide down into the throat to gargle with, swishing them back and forth in the mouth, and then she spat them back out onto the ground.

When Ardrogna approached her again the day after her return to the village, Cristina was almost terse, but generous, as Ardrogna had never seen her.

—Me confuse, much move-round mind, much move-round chest. Now me back with Rosie-old. Me stay with Rosie-old. Thank you help Rosie-old.

Cristina and Rosie went around their work – the

tortilleria in the morning, cleaning, cooking, tending to the cows and the tomatoes, and then the night.

Behind their house, ants lifted scraps of food onto their rears. A bee landed on a stalk of bristly purple buds on the tree in front of the sisters' house, poised clumsily, fell. Its legs clutched at the air for a few seconds before it righted itself and found its way back onto the stalk.

The dogs and cats lay in the shade all day. The small tan dog that ate Rosie and Cristina's leftovers gasped in the middle of the day when it was hottest, and the lines of his ribs shook with each gasp. With much exertion, he lifted his head every time someone passed by him to lick at the air half-heartedly before his head dropped back onto the ground.

The tan dog's brother had stopped eating the week before and his breaths came shuddering and irregular. When he stopped licking at the water that Cristina set down in a shallow flowered dish at his nose, she threw a rubber mat over him so he could die under it without flies bothering him. The lump under the black rubber trembled whenever the dog took a big mouthful of air.

The grey dog down the road whose lower eyelids showed red and sad collapsed into the dust-pile next to the fence in the morning, sending motes up to hover in the light, and stayed curled up there until nightfall, when people tossed their leftovers out. Always, she lay with her long nose under her back legs. Sometimes her eyes opened when a car went by, but it did not often happen.

The two tabby cats that lived in the yard kept their paws around each other's necks. When they were not sleeping or washing together, they sat on their haunches with their eyes glistening in expectation and ears back, waiting until one sprung forward to claw at the other. Sometimes they went off on their own and sat like fat old men, small front paws resting on furry, rounded chests.

Cristiano, the little boy from next door, held two fingers up behind Rosie's head in a 'V' sign as she emptied the dustpan in the road; she did not see and Cristiano brightened with glee at his victory.

Everything was much the same as it had always been, except that Ismael was not there.

But just when Cristina had started to believe that things would stay this way, that she had conquered her restless need to throw a pebble into the lake of her indeterminate ennui, there came a few minutes in a long, stiflingly hot day. She was sitting on the top step outside the stone house, catching her breath after cutting down the weeds and overgrowth from the piece of land they owned out past the edges of town.

Neidi came strolling by, her firm rounds of flesh held

up by her purple dress, and a warm smile grew on her face; Cristina stayed in the oasis of that smile for a few minutes.

Idly, she watched a few of the rusted farm trucks so familiar to her go by. The pistons of the old, loyal engines worked hard as the trucks clang-banged down the road, hands waving from the backs, roped-up chairs sliding in the pan, exhaust puffing from the pipe as it would from a railroad.

But here was a glaring black, low-riding car that by its presence terrorized the mild road with its fading paint and the dogs curled on the dirt and the gaggle of barefoot children in their athletic shorts and T-shirts, hitting a pink rubber ball with a thick branch.

Cristina craned her neck to see who could be driving this car, so alien to the village. The tinted window on the driver's side was lowered a few inches, and through it Cristina saw a green and yellow snake eye looking straight at her with menacing disdain. The car slowed as it drove past their house, and the man did not take his eyes off Cristina till he was out of range. She now saw that the skin had been pitted by various sicknesses. He wanted her to know that he was watching her and Rosie and that, whenever he or his bosses pleased, he could punish them for what Ismael had done.

She thought of Ismael, away from the village he had

spent his entire life in and alone in an unfamiliar place where he would not be able to tell people what he thought or felt – Ismael, always smooth and easy at the centre of things. Even without knowing that it was just the day before that the pot-bellied man had seized her brother by his throat, she felt his agitation.

Her thoughts fled from her again, for the first time since she had returned to the village from her days with the tiger-kerchief man. In her stomach an antenna with a sucker on its end awakened that refused to detach from minutiae. It vacuumed in everything in sight, the debris rattling around in the emptiness, creating raucous diversion before all went quiet and it went seeking again. It made Cristina hungry, and she took increasingly larger, devouring bites out of her life with Rosie, like a fish drinking the briny water it lived in. The water was running out.

She did not look for the scorpion tattooed man or ask anyone about him. She knew when it was best for her to place something outside of the immediate reach of her body, because nothing in her life had given her any way of truly understanding the thing or how to manage it. These things were far, far away. The fingers folded down against the palm, and then the whole hand turned upwards in one solid, fluid movement, the fingers turning heaven-ward, to send whatever it was you were talking about into space, to rest with the other perpetual mysteries that lived there.

Cristina held onto the plastic wind-up dog so tightly that the legs left red marks in her palm that would not fade till a few days had passed.

And the next time she was in the big store, she pointed at the plastic hexagonal canister where the single cigarettes honeycombed. Another thing that Ismael had not tolerated, another thing that she had never done. The tarry smoke plugged her chest and streamed out of her mouth with a whoosh, and the flecked orange end burned a black hole through the skin on the dark of Ismael's room.

Every night Cristina sat in Ismael's bedroom and struck a match to light a cigarette, letting the velvety ash peak on the floor. The next morning, Rosie swept the cold remnants away.

Chapter Six

Without being able to sit in front of the store in the evening light and see where one thing lay in relation to another as he sipped a cold Victoria beer with Jose, Ismael did not know where his mind stopped and the world began, or the other way round. It was not something he had ever questioned before. The separation had been clear and distinct.

For a few days after he saw the photo of the green-eyed woman in the car, Ismael saw vestiges of what had happened after the fiesta spill from him and alight into the vast, unknown city. They took shape against the blank screen of the side of a tall building; they came onto the stage of the luncheria counter as he munched on enchiladas, a Coca-Cola by his side. Then they flew back into him, and swooped hastily out again like bats. Their tiny talons grazed over Ismael's shoulder and caught in his hair.

The quicksilver transformation from desire into violence of that night, the acute recognition of the man's malodorous flesh in Ismael's own as he brought the gun up and shot, the slackening of grudging family histories he had not known were still alive in him during the long walk back to the village from the cantina, collapsing into the past, his efforts to pin everything down where he could see it all like fireflies on a board, and, most of all, his agonizing failure to understand anything that had happened. The scathing taste of bile stayed in his mouth. Later, it became a stone in his gut, and nausea churned around it. Everything around him seemed distant and everything distant seemed close by.

It all mixed together and apparitions tumbled down on him. They were the only thing Ismael could see, but despite their presence he knew he had to try to find another job. He put one foot in front of the other and walked straight into the shadows without protection. After a day or two of walking up and down the mountain, the net loosening minutely with each step, he became strong enough to cut the threads of the mesh that his interior mess was trying to spin around him. His feet were freed from their path up and down the mountain and they took him to the now familiar *mercado*, and he found a new job.

The last time, the boss had led him straight to the place he was to work; but this time, a paper with squiggly lines was handed to Ismael. He did not understand, and he told this to his new boss with a shrug and a finger pointed at himself, then two hands held upright on either side of the chest. Even the people here understood what this meant.

One of the other men at the job would be here in the *mercado* the next morning and Ismael could go with him to the job, he saw when his new boss with the purplish-whitish pouches under his eyes pointed to the skinny man with a pompadour and aviator shades and then to Ismael, then held his two forefingers together. He pointed to an invisible watch and held one palm and one finger up: six a.m..

Ismael knew the sun would wake him in plenty of time. The next morning, the first light came through the thickness of his sleep, but he defied it and stayed underwater for a little more time before he swam up through the sleek calm and awoke.

The man in aviator shades led him down a road lined with animal-feed stores, stacked plastic-weave bags, some of them spilling grainy seed, and sapphire and jade parakeets, wings beating the air in cages above them. Up this way past the fabric shop with its rolls of flowered vinyl and gingham at the corner, and a right, by way of a small thoroughfare with adobe arches, behind each plastic-covered clothes hanging from wire hangers all the way up to the ceiling, handmade Maya traditional dresses bordered with blossoms and vines that stabbed Ismael with longing for his sisters and the village, and mass-manufactured polyester football jerseys and stiff pairs of jeans, bouquets of neon plastic keychains in front.

Then they were out into a cobblestoned square. The man pointed to the opposite end to tell Ismael that was where they were working, but Ismael was mesmerized by a group around a few tables at their end of the square. Hands rose and established themselves into foreign patterns that stitched the disparate world together in a way Ismael had not seen since leaving home.

The Mexican sign language used here in the city was different from the regional Mayan sign language dialect used in the village, as different as Spanish is from spoken Mayan. And Ismael had never left the village and had no experience of picking up another language. Yet there was a core alertness to the physical shape of things that helped him sense what the group was talking about.

Everything in his starving, desperate body turned towards the group, but Ismael had spent his very last few coins on his morning cup of Nescafé bought from the old pear-shaped woman. There had been no chilaquiles that morning, nor anything the day before.

The two hungers competed fiercely, and the one that yearned for human contact that would show him again where the boundaries of his self lay was winning easily. Then

Ismael thought about what his father had asked him to do all those years before, and he wrenched himself away from the sight of the group and followed the man across the square to work.

His child's eyes, bewildered and bright, stayed on the group. Ismael had deaf eyes, and a craggy, hook-nosed woman with bright pink in her earlobes saw that with one glance and waved to him. He waved back, but he forced himself to walk past.

He was pulled along inexorably through the day as he hauled cement blocks from a pile on one side of a dusty, parched lot through the dormant, loitering air to another pile on the other side of the lot, his knuckles red and bleeding.

Ismael's mind was filled with the hands he had seen that morning. When they were finished for the day and the men went as always to the corner shop for a beer, Ismael ran back to the square, but they were not there.

Every morning now he looked for them, and the nights were not so dark or so long. His delusions left for the cave where they roosted, in row after row of folded tissue, tenuous brown and grey blooms stuck like barnacles to the roof of the cave, their foul-smelling droppings building up into rock formations on the floor.

One night after work, Ismael wanted for the first time

97

to enter the church at the bottom of the road that led up the mountain to his lean-to. He had felt too polluted even to look at it before.

The main doors were open and fluorescent strip lights were switched on against the night and the insects. Teenagers in their neon shirts leant against the cement walls or sat in the dark-wood pews, hands in tight jean pockets, but they did not forget their chaperone. The Virgin of Guadalupe looked down from pennants, letters cut from felt, ceramic figurines, and a subtle painting by Omar Salamanca Lopez stood in the main altar against the back wall. In front of the altar were rows of flaming candles, each one a secret prayer.

Ismael had gone to church every week with his mother and then with Rosie after his mother died. His eyes always strayed to the pretty women watching so intently and earnestly. Here, it was the same, and the women were exotic and even prettier to him. But when entering and exiting the room, in the middle of flirting or laughing, every person turned to touch forehead, heart, shoulder, shoulder, and then to kiss the hand that held all, and finally they clutched their hands to their chest, to try to put all they hoped and asked from Guadalupe and the church, into their hearts.

In the village it had been one gesture among many. In the city, it was for these movements that Ismael started going to the church every evening after his one beer with the men. You saw the sign all over the city, but it was concentrated at the church.

Ismael sat quietly in the pews, meeting no one's eyes, snatching onto the gesture every time he saw it and swallowing it deep. Like the sight of the group of deaf people, the gesticulation pushed Ismael further away from the edge and reminded him of the border between his frail husk and the unknowable world that housed him. He tried to paint the knowledge permanently onto the walls of his mind.

A few weeks after he began going to the church, Ismael saw the hook-nosed deaf woman with pink stars in her ears sitting alone at the table where he had first seen her. He ran to her and she looked up, remembering him and those dark, quick moving eyes of his. He patted down on the space around him and shrugged; where are they? She answered with fluidity in her hands, and with it she pulled thick strands of contaminated blood from Ismael. He did not follow everything she said, but he understood that he was to come back to the square that night.

Another day of moving concrete blocks, and pollo quesadillas bought from a woman whose eyes, seeing inside herself rather than outside, made Ismael think of Rosie, after which he walked eagerly to the square. The tables were filled with conjuring hands and arms. The eyes had expressions that harmonized with Ismael's own.

In the centre of the group was a squat, thick-bodied woman about the same age as Cristina. The certainty in her body and the penetrating quality of her eyes was heightened in her gestures.

Tippity-tap, tippity-tap, tippity-tap . . . her wee sausages of pinky fingers went up and down, up and down against the legs of her stool, but then her other fingers joined into the jig, and finally her clumsy wallflower thumbs dared to hop in. They exchanged partners, swung out and back in, and gathered together to the same beat, clap, clap down on the wood of the stool their owner sat on. One hand clenched in front of the composed mouth, then the fist was opened and the fingers spread to pour from her lips, followed by the other hand. The river of her hands diverged for each hand to go into opposite directions. She closed both fists again, but now when they opened it was with a quick, hard motion that fragmented the river she had just made. She continued to fragment it for some time, and with the last shattering motion she let her hands fade into space.

Her hands softened when they went as far as they could. They turned upwards and swept towards her chest as they moved inwards slowly. As her hands reached her breasts, they moulded all together until she had a whole again. She put her hands out one last time to make sure she had gotten all the crumbs onto the ball. Finally, she put it down to roll away.

Ismael stepped up impatiently to her after she finished, wanting to be close to the first person he had seen since leaving the village who used the movements of her body to purify, as Jose did. He had the talent of finding a faithful rhyme in his body for concrete things, and the even rarer ability to transmit the shape of emotions and the anonymous in a way that Ismael felt the truth of. Without understanding the sign language that the woman used, Ismael saw she did this. He knew, in the same way that anyone sees the gesture made in devotion to the Virgin and knows the sincerity of it.

She nodded curtly to Ismael when he flapped his hand at her and pointed at his ear to tell her that he was also deaf. She had plenty of other people grouped around her, wanting to pay homage. He was just one more, and he did not look Mexican.

In some dismay, he turned back to the woman with pink at her ears, and she smiled; she understood when he told her in rudimentary gestures that he had recently come to the city from a small village with a different sign language. She told him in a similar way that she was from here, from this city, and that she worked squeezing orange juice in one of the stalls in the *mercado*. Her name sign was Beak-nose, for her hook nose, and her husband had left her for another woman not too long ago.

Some of the other people he met that night understood him better than others did. In none of them did he find what he had in the village; the thorough sureness in the body and the complete ease with one another. After a little while, he understood that none of them had known each other a lifetime. They had grown up in a house where their parents and the people around them did not know their language, and even now, they spent most of their lives not understanding and not being understood. But Ismael drank thirstily of what came out of their hands and arms. And now he knew where and when to find them. He was stronger for the knowledge.

He stayed in the square with them until the last person went home. The long trudge up the mountain and past the houses with lights in the windows, telling of people going around their lives with each other, was less lonely than it had been the day before.

The next day after work, he turned up and down the crowded passages of the *mercado*, the ripe scent of drying beef hanging overhead from metal racks filling his nostrils, piles of plastic toys and trinkets arousing his curiosity, until he saw Beak-nose behind a corner stall. She squeezed orange juice for him, pressing the halved spheres between metal plates and running the bright liquid into a cup for Ismael. The rinds lay on the counter turned inside out to white, their holy water drunk and observed.

He went back to see her as often as he could, and before another week went by, they clung to each other in his red hammock and he told her, as he had so often told himself, of the magnificence of the jungle beneath them, of their singular position up above it all. And this time, he believed it quickly and much more fully.

He started coming to the rented room that Beak-nose shared with her sister, who could hear but gestured to Ismael to tell him about the dirty streets she walked through to and from her job in a nail salon, painting nails in smooth, careful strokes, and of the choking, chemical fumes she breathed all day long.

After work, he ran up the metal steps through the clinging heat to their room, past the terrace where they sometimes cooked. Beak-nose was always there in front of the electric burners next to the mattresses on the painted concrete floor. Their beans with lard bubbled and beef *fileteada* sizzled and tortillas hardened in the purple pots and pans Beak-nose had brought home from the *mercado*.

Ismael still had the taste of the village and his sisters in his mouth all the time; but now he could taste other things too. Some of the feelings left him like a fart, bringing relief to an overextended condition.

He had found a way to endure the city, Ismael thought. When he lugged the concrete blocks, he felt that his sweat forced out the residue of that night at the fiesta. He saw it, the white around the necks of his T-shirts turning the palest yellow. He saw the sediment and the grains of dirt appearing between the ribs of the cloth. It came from inside him.

Yet the green-eyed woman was alive in him, much more alive than Beak-nose, lying next to him in his hammock, her chapped hands moving slowly up and down the sides of his chest, her sturdy legs nestled between his skinny ones just before they fell asleep. Her thin lips made the shape they always did when she liked what he was doing to her. The mouth pulled inward and then out again, ending in a round O, but it was not her face that he saw.

When the corrosive questions about the green-eyed woman and that night flared up again, nothing had changed. The bitterness was still in his chest and it was hot and un-relenting.

Ismael moved between his day-to-day life in the city, in which the past did not torment in the way it had, and the astringent region in his chest for a long time, but they never dripped into each other. He lashed everything down in each territory as tightly as he could.

One day, his eye was drawn to some posters printed with strips of pink, green and purple that seemed to have been plastered everywhere: to the side of the *mercado*, all around the cobblestoned square he walked through to get to work, the inside wall of the pear-shaped old woman's restaurant, even the Catholic church. The pastel layers of torn flyers faded one into the next like tints of chalk blended together, divided by echelons of white strata, peeling raggedly down to the history of the layer beneath that, like cliff faces in the desert.

He scanned the accumulation of mysterious markings beneath the recognizable drawing of a bull and toreador. Variously: *'Plaza de Toros; Caletilla; Si el tiempo no le impide y con permiso de la autoridad; Gran corrida de toros de feria una brillante banda de musica amenizara el spectaculo; Precios y de mas detalles; En programas de mano; Seis hermosos toros; Domino Ortega y Manuel Rodriguez Manolete y Carlos Arruza'* and below, a clear date and time. Ismael had seen the bullring at the foot of the steep hill with the ruins of the old fortress on top, and he decided to go to the fight.

When the ticket-seller asked for money with a raised forefinger and thumb, curved, held horizontally, and rubbed against one another, Ismael proffered a few pesos. The carnation-pink ticket he got in return swiftly went to the pockmarked, eagle-eyed teenager at the entrance to the bullring.

The ring had a palm frond roof of daggered brown and poles lashed together. Ladders led up to the second tier where spectators sat on folding chairs doubly rowed, the children on the floor near the front, legs hanging over the edge.

Around the ring, Ismael could smell kaleidoscoped scents of white flour dough crisping in spattering oil, the earthy acidity of red-edged, opaline-centred radish garnishes sprinkled over with cilantro, lime being squeezed, drinks tables of beer and tequila concoctions, red chilli powder sprinkled over corn cobs on sticks, tacos dribbling oil onto paper plates, churros to be dusted with cinnamon sugar and bagged in greaseproof paper with the sweet grains gathering in the corners, paper-lined aluminium pans high with taquitos of shredded chicken to be poured over with soured cream and covered with shredded lettuce, avocado and tomato slices, and crumbled cheese.

Ismael watched as a man in a faded baseball cap with a Mexican flag on it tried to snatch a beer from a cooler in front of Ismael as he walked past it. Then he was on the ground, beer back in the vendor's cooler, the hard raised heel of a boot in his face, the other boot in his stomach above the oval leather cowhide buckle of his belt. The vendor's eyes kept looking at the same unfathomable place.

Walking past the man and up into the second tier of the ring, Ismael settled into his seat and followed the path of the tequila from the ice in his plastic glass to his belly. He lowered the brim of his protective baseball cap to mark his place among the more macho cowboy hats and collared shirts framing outspread chests all around him. In the ring, a round-cheeked toddler with limpid eyes of mahogany gripped the horn of the saddle in front of his proud grand-father as their palomino horse, orange ribbons woven into its mane, sauntered loose hipped around the ring.

As the boy retreated into the warm lap of his mother, the bird of paradise matador entered the ring where the bull waited, to ready the crowd for their dance.

The gold buttons on each trouser leg of the matador caught the light, and the pink of Manuel Rodriguez Manolete's cloak goaded as he leapt around the ring, landing on tiptoes before spinning and drawing the bull in another direction. The black, matted fur against the flamboyant pink and yellow silk; the round, dark eye and the squinted, strategic one; the dense horn and hooves aligned with the flying manoeuvres.

An old crone saluted her ancient, solemn *vaquero* when the knife went in the first time and she was rewarded with a crack of a smile.

As the matador dislodged the collective inertia and sorrow with arcing, bowing brandishes of the cape, Ismael succumbed. It was at this instant of giving way, when his tied down emotions loosened, that the green-eyed woman entered into his eyesight again.

She was across the arena from Ismael, and she was alone. Her white dress had puffed sleeves, with a plum-coloured ribbon bow tied around each arm. Another ribbon tied in front, pushing together the breasts that Ismael dreamed about. His eyes fed on her fully. Again he discovered the startling, verdant green of her eyes as they cast downwards, and he had forgotten the shape shifts of her small nose when it turned to the side. He had memorized her face so exactly that he could see that in the relatively short time since he had last seen her, the curve of her cheeks had slightly eroded. He saw that she would not age like Rosie, whittled to purity, nor would the structure of her face be ground down into bagginess like in Cristina. Her face would smooth into a new cohesion of features.

He downed his drink, tapping the bottom to send the last of the tequila winding idly into his mouth. In front of him, dappled horses blurred through the sawdust, carrying men with them; the vitality of the action consoled. It was not enough to prevent the brittle deposit that had slowly built up inside Ismael since the fiesta from crumbling.

Through the jangling noise of everything going through him; through the hectic clattering of the feelings and questions bumping off the walls of Ismael's psyche, screeching unearthly and burbling like a hairless newborn; through all of it, a single urge drove clean and sharp. Ismael got to his feet to go to her. She had not seen him.

He pushed through the crowd, shoving aside impulses in his pursuit, as the bull charged in the ring. The bulk of both man and bull could see only purpose in this moment.

The fine powder thrown up by the hooves of the bull entered Ismael's frail, receptive nostrils and intoxicated him into a trance of longing for the woman. All that had happened since he had last seen her, everything that the brief contact with her had shaken loose from the foundations of his life, only made his desire stronger now.

A string threaded through his chin jerked his head up like a marionette's to look at the woman. She was not alone any longer. The pregnant-bellied, weak-jawed man from the car was next to her. Seeing them together now, Ismael saw that something in the man's manner was similar to the man he had killed. Maybe the pregnant-bellied man was his replacement. Ismael's rampaging instincts were jarringly stilled.

Even through the treacly musk cologne of the men, the shrill flowery perfumes the women wore, the replete oiliness of the food, the wheat of the animals and the straw tossed down on the dung, and the smoggy car exhaust that over-laid all other smells, Ismael knew he would have been able to smell the intimacy of lovers if it lay between them, but it was not there. Neither was the certainty of a family con-nection. His vision was a dirty smudge, but he smelled something chemical and artificial between them. It was business, he felt more than ever.

Ismael pushed brutally down on the need to be next to the woman. The fiendish intruder was driven into his nucleus, and he buried it well, padded and insulated it. He did not know how long it would stay there. He changed direction, his feet carrying his head over the pole floor, weak under his feet; down the square cut through the floor of the second tier of the ring, and clambering onto the shaky ladder to the first floor of the bullring.

She was out of the faintest periphery of his vision, and he was surrounded by unknown people. People he knew as well as he knew anyone.

He thought again of leaving the city. It had taken all of himself to set up here in the city, and the thought of packing up his things and his hammock and going to another strange place where he did not know the streets and the faces to look for yet another job was overwhelmingly sapping. Again, he felt sure that they would find him anywhere he could muster up the courage to go. He could not go back to the village, and if he could not be there he did not attach importance to his life.

And the green-eyed woman's beauty and allure was undiminished.

He did not go to Beak-nose's room that night to tell her about the bullfight, as he had told her he would. The next day, he did, but to say that he could not see her any longer. To her tearful, angry questions why, he said only that more of his past was here in the city than he had known.

Ismael knew he had to unknot some of it, but he did not know how.

The spectres of Rosie and Cristina became his only steady companions again.

He still went to see the deaf people in the square, but with no regularity.

Every day after work, he went into the church and looked for the gesture. He owed nothing to the people who made it, unlike with the deaf people in the square. When he saw the gesture, it did not soothe him by blanketing everything else. It invoked what things were made of and how they fit together, or didn't fit together. It soaked up what the green-eyed woman and the men had left behind in Ismael; its accuracy took in the excess energies that had nowhere to go. There was just as much unruliness around Ismael, and he did not know any more about how it would end. All he knew was that it would end one way or the other. But more was made present, and then more was made absent, leaving temporary room in his clogged body.

The apparitions that had haunted him stayed roosting in their dank cave. Occasionally Ismael felt or smelled an intense trace of them, but he wrestled them to the ground and did not allow them to blind him.

Chapter Seven

Rosie sat on the speckled cement of the bottom step in front of the house. The heat fell down on her, she stretched her chicken legs in front of her, and the heat sank into her mind.

Inside chest float float float need float. Better ignore all around, not look up not look around. Me Rosie-old me not look. Not understand not look. Me Rosie-old me calm calm better better look away. Inside chest it different. Feel will explode something explode inside something something can't stop.

Something had shifted under them in the village, and maybe under Ismael wherever he was. Rosie felt it. She had been happy when Cristina came back, and everything had almost been the way it had always been. Rosie did her work and she watched the beetles hiding in the damp safety of the fallen leaves that piled up, cradling newly dropped twigs. The onyx backs of the beetles glinted blackly through the crackly dullness of the leaves, like a baby thinking nobody can see her because she cannot see anyone.

Cristina's brown eyes were as tender as a cow's for many weeks. They opened up and they made the rest of her face mild. But then everything in her face had been pounded together. The pale brown dots on her cheeks were stale breadcrumbs on a dirty floor, and the wide mouth had just tasted something sour.

Rosie knew when Cristina had changed again. It happened when she saw the malicious man with the strange eye who had been at the fiesta that night, standing next to the beautiful, sly woman Ismael loved.

Rosie was not afraid of the man. But she had seen the scorpions tattooed on his forearms. He had rested them on the steering wheel of his ugly car when it drove in front of their house. And a few minutes later, she had seen a scorpion twitch and disappear from the room as she stood at her hammock loom.

She did not know if the scorpion was real or in her mind. Either way, it existed and it made her anxious. Her entire self focused on keeping everything secure in its place, in the same way as the scorpion lives to sting. She had the strength of the tree she saw in her mind. Even though she knew all would not be permanently shattered and that her siblings would come back to her, she had to push with every drop of her potency to keep things where she knew they should be.

The top branch in the back divide of the hog's pen had once been wood through and through, but now it only appeared to be. Maggots laid eggs in the centre of the limb. The sightless blobs ate outwards, chewing the gristly white strands with gusto, until only a thin band of fibre remained below the brown grain of the branch. One more alteration in the atmosphere would be a cue for movement, most of it subtle, but some overt and fundamental, in the maggots, in the mat of scorpions outside town, the smog of ravens in their tree, the bats having a kip upside down in their cave, the beetles scrabbling in the dirt, the lizards darting to and fro over the boughs, and the blown-up fruit in the foliage.

Rosie had never felt so many creatures congregate upon the village. They had stayed in dens scattered over the terrain, in nests only seen arbitrarily, shrubbery that did not encroach. Now, much was either crowding in or escaping. Rosie did not wonder why this was or if other people saw it. It was not in her nature or in her language. She had always known deeply that it was possible for a sharp phenomenon to crack the thin shell of lassitude that protected the village and everyone in it. That was the potential of what was there, in the world and in humanity. Enough had changed in their lives in recent months to remind her again and again of it.

She forced her eyes open to see in front of her, hoping that what was inside her head would dim and she would see that it was not real after all. Then maybe the world would align itself. But her mind and the world were equally lucid and sentient, and the possibility that she feared was there in both.

Her hope was the nebulous, flushed streak of light between the world and her mind. She concentrated everything on the sparkling divider. Slowly, slowly, the sheet rose and thickened. A red-hot synthesis of the remnants of Rosie's strength cooled. The wall was more opaque than it had been.

Trepidation arrived a few seconds later and filled out when Cristina entered the room to stand beside Rosie, and her stout hand reached for Rosie's forehead. It seemingly rested there, but as the hand lay on her, Rosie felt the prickliness and aggression in her sister's lumbering fingers become vigorous. She felt it go inside her, and she felt her sister clumsily but effectively remove the illumine dividing Rosie's psyche from what lay around them.

Cristina, Cristina . . . Even after everything, she could not be still. She had to disturb, to agitate, to free something into the world that made sense of what was inside her and what had been inside of her grandmother. Cristina knew how to make it happen through her sister who held so little of her own self in her chest, and instead so much of the world around them. Rosie could not stop it.

Cristina threw the pane outside Rosie, stamped on it, and the crystal glass shattered, broken into luminescent diamonds that rolled all over the ground. One spun straight down into the right leg of the plastic chair Rosie sat on and lodged there, where it glittered with defiant ridicule.

Rosie saw a brown carapace shaping into a body and bursting down and out into tail and legs, and finally curving outwards into mandibles until the scorpion she had seen in the room was lying undeniably in her injured psyche. She knew it could not hurt her, would never hurt her, but it would hurt other people. It began to move.

In the pigs' pen, the top branch fell to the ground and the slimy, unsighted maggots swarmed out as the scorpion crawled out of Rosie through her unused ear canal where the little hairs had never grown, and the scorpion fell on its back onto the hard dirt to claw angrily at the air, then scrambled to right itself.

The dirt roads were black with beetles, wing to wing, echoing the paillettes of tar on the roads in the big city. Bird corpses lay on top of them in tatters of scarlet and feather being eaten rapidly to bone. Only the eagles, who were prey to no other bird, remained in the trees. A truck carrying Coca-Cola to the store opposite the house with a blue drawing of a cow on it flattened some maggots into a white paste and drove insensibly on.

Cristina huddled on a small wooden stool just outside the room where Rosie sat in the green plastic basket chair by the door. The contaminated, metallic sheen of her eyes leaked down wetly onto the floor till her eyes were emptied of any expression. She stared in on her older sister from another realm. Her mouth no longer tasted something sour, but instead crushed in shame at what she knew she could not undo. Rosie would never be safe in her separate world again. Cristina lit cigarette after cigarette, until the ash made a moat around her, like the natural one that had disappeared from around Rosie's essentiality.

Rosie stayed in her chair and kept her eyes shut. She knew she could not let Cristina or any of them claw at her. She did not want to see, or even more dangerous, talk to any person. She could not answer questions or make what had happened into a story; she did not know what had happened. The current of conversation could pull her under.

And enough had crept out of her mind by virtue of other people's soiled hands.

Something had melted in her and was shivering. She had to protect it the best she could. Ismael was not here to protect her.

Pink and white threads from the hammock Rosie had recently started stretched from side to side in the room. Above her hung a swaying light bulb suspended by a black electrical cord, and its light made a circle on the cement floor.

Calm calm now calm me Rosie-old need calm. Need focus fix inside need all settle down inside. Scorpion out run run around scorpion out run run around prick poison prick prick poison.

Precariousness injected itself like a spider's egg sac under the facades of Cristina's days, and the eggs hatched.

Her days had always been broken up by spatters of gossip or of laughter and teasing, but these were only momentary interruptions in the wide, smooth mass of silence. Like a child in front of a white wall, she tried her best to graffiti it over with cartoonish marks; like a child, she ran away and tried to stay away for as long as she could. But in the end it closed over everything dropped into it.

Now, Cristina needed and even wanted silence as she never had. It was the only refuge she could hope for now that she had completely fallen into her urge to destroy. She wished fervently to disappear into silence, but of course, just when she wanted it wretchedly, it was more elusive than it had ever been.

The plastic dog was still a reassuring lump in her pocket, but it seemed pathetic where it had not before.

After the day she reached injuriously into Rosie – she had seen something she had never seen before and wanted to touch the glinting entity, she did not understand the impulse any further than that – nameless things nipped at her, pulling her away from what was in front of her. It pounded down and down on her and she felt the earth's pulsations beneath her feet. She was being buffeted from above and below, and from inside as a hammering tremor grew.

It was relentless. The trees twisted as restlessly as she now did. The sky was a pale grey, and it seemed much closer to her than usual.

But she found her way out of it and into oblivion.

The dogs and cats snapped and clawed at the beetles at first, batting the corpses back and forth between their paws before depositing them at Rosie's feet, but presently the insects ran audaciously over their snouts. The animals' bellies were full with birds; first it had been gratifying, but now they waited again for the more exotically flavoured human leftovers.

Almost every person in the village had seen a scorpion in the last few days, but nobody had been bitten. The old men drinking their Victoria beer in front of the store remarked on it in their gossip, but it quickly slid over them and was buried. Pestilence and misfortune were daily occurrences and the weather had been irregular; that would bring the creatures.

The biggest scorpion of all, the one that had crept out of Rosie, lay in the lean-to, its body hissing with suppressed toxin. Its tail whipped through the air when Cristina walked near it on her way to the outhouse to empty her queasy stomach. Seeing it, Cristina saw an easy chance to remedy some of the guilt she felt. She moved her squat big toe closer and closer to its secateurs and her thick, yellowed, over-hanging toenail came up and shoved at the scorpion roughly. It would not let her off that quick, and it rightfully bit her. Its sloshing serum entered Cristina's chubby leg, and a red blotch grew outwards from a bloody pinprick in the centre. The red sore spot of the sting throbbed comfortingly; she would not have to think about anything else for a few minutes.

The venom wriggled up and into Cristina with hilarity, shooting fast into tendrils that unrolled down her blood vessels.

A violent, contracting rattling started in Cristina's deserted body before it quieted into jittery shakes. Chit, chit, chit her muscles snapped and shook slower, slower before finally Cristina slumped onto the floor in the lean-to. Sweat dripped down her tainted body. All became one for her, and she receded into it thankfully.

Rosie tended faithfully to her, washing Cristina with fresh water and a sponge several times a day, smoothing over her chapped, cracked lips with petroleum jelly, and trickling bottled water slowly down her throat. She summoned Juan-Deafy and Neidi to help lift Cristina's dead weight into her hammock. Through her daze, Cristina felt the departure from the gritty dust of the dirt floor of the lean-to and the entrance into the lissom, buoyant position that the hammock made possible. Opening her eyes briefly, she crumpled into relief at the sight of Neidi and clung to her feverishly; the brown eyes that lingered on Neidi's were as abandoned of rationale and direction as a sheep's. Neidi saw, and she did not attempt to lead Cristina anywhere.

Soon Cristina fell back into sweet, hot nothingness.

Ardrogna came to see the patient, and relished seeing the filth that clouded over Cristina and the cocoon of aloofness that Rosie lived in when not nursing her sister. Soon the whole village knew where Ardrogna thought the sisters found themselves. Ardrogna talked on and on to everyone she met; she did not want anyone to brush her words away and look at what was under them. She was a bug under a rock that had never been turned over.

There was no doctor in the village. There was a small medical clinic up behind Juan-Deafy's hut; one of the people who had come to study the language of the villagers had donated money to build it and keep it supplied. Chabelo the tailor had been put in charge of the fund. He had talked lengthily and seemingly with honour about the need for health care in the village. The first doctor who came from the city had stayed a year, and then the money that was supposed to last indefinitely had run out. Chabelo said the gringo had miscalculated how much was necessary, but everyone in the village saw the new red pickup truck parked in front of Chabelo's house. The comisario, the appointed political leader of the village, saw it too; but that kind of thing happened all the time and there was never any proof.

Now, the clinic stood empty, its back wall used as a place for secret assignations. The native medicine had long been forgotten, in the same way that the carvings from the old temple in the jungle outside the village had been taken away by people who came in Jeeps. The nearest doctor was three hours away and the villagers only went to him if someone endured a very long and peculiar illness. All other ailments of the mind, body and spirit were treated with a sponge over the body, a blanket wrapped tightly around, and hordes of people surrounding the patient, bumping and shoving and talking.

Rosie did not let them crowd into the house. They came one or two at a time or not at all. When not attending to Cristina or keeping the house clean and herself fed, she sat in the main room of the house on the green plastic chair, with the door closed and the fan on. The cool air streamed over her hot skin. If a hand waved over the horizontal shutters of the glassless window, she peered cautiously outside to see who it was and how many there were.

Cristina stayed submerged in the welcome murkiness. The guilt and plaguing knowledge of her uselessness dissipated. There was only a vague sense that an infinitesimal fraction of the weight of the world belonged to her and was her responsibility, as it is for every person.

But at the universal bottom of the fluctuating haze of coma, as if through gradations of consciousness, Cristina still felt the crustacean body of a scorpion and the presence of a hypnotizing, repellent fear. And in the days that followed, whenever she came up to the surface briefly and saw the room she lay in, the apocalyptic fear coated everything and she dived fast back into her sickness.

Around her inert body, the new days came with new strength.

The last of the beetles lay still on the road. Cars and feet mashed them into the forgotten.

The maggots squirmed on the hard dirt of the hogs' pen, opalescent bodies squashing in the middle to nudge forward, head by tail by head, first one and then the other, making a marathon trek across a vast desert. They reached various wet oases, met a valley of dragons in the sharp hog hooves that eliminated many, had their juices sucked up by the unapologetic sun, leaving them dry and crumbly.

A toddler with arms and legs like plump sausages squealed for her pet baby goat. It had run away, the frayed rope around its neck trailing on the dirt. Tottering after it, she awakened a chocolate-brown scorpion loitering under the table in her house and it stung, then scurried away like a slightly bigger, uglier cockroach. Her mother, grandmother, aunts and sisters crowded around in their bright embroidered dresses with lace skirts underneath, to wail and pray and later, to put her into the ground.

Nobody had seen any evidence of the scorpions since then, except for Rosie. As she sat beside her sister, her mind was living in a locked, veiled room of grainy ambiguity from which she observed the village as if from above.

Rosie's insides settled as the creatures retreated from the village. The first frightening scorpion had come after Ismael had left; after Cristina saw the green-eyed woman and her two soldiers at the fiesta. Rosie's corporeal psyche sensed the reverberation in their surroundings and in Cristina's equilibrium. These things were not to be encapsulated by explaining away in any way, not that she had that urge or ability. No emotional parallels were marked; no carefully built up infrastructure was obliterated; no responsibility was ascribed according to superstitions, ancient or mechanical.

The movement and energy was there around them, that was all.

Rosie compelled her insides to stop shivering. The melted stuff had evaporated; and now it was coming back down into her. Rosie crystallized the purity and kept the malevolence at a distance. She would cosset herself always now, even more strongly, and weave between herself and Cristina so that Cristina would not be able to reach into her again. But maybe Cristina's illness would cure Cristina of that. Maybe the poison would go from Rosie. Rosie hoped, even as she felt she was damaged and weakened for good.

Rosie had to make sure that their blood and vulnerability was not fed off so easily. Ismael had done that before he himself was preyed on. Rosie knew Ismael would come back, but it was too late for her.

She dipped a clean cloth into the pail of water in front of her and wrung it out, then mopped Cristina's forehead with it.

Outside the house, cumbersome grey clouds erased the drowsiness like a sponge over a powdery chalkboard. All the animals sat upright, sniffing the air nervously. The bugs hid away in their labyrinthine tunnels; the women hurriedly swept all the washing down from the lines crisscrossing the village and heaped it into the hammocks to fold later.

Children left their games and ran into the nearest open doorway; men who had been sitting on their stoops retreated into their houses and shut all the doors and windows.

The rain came all at once and the dust that covered everything became mud. Small dents in the road that you barely noticed when you walked over them turned into lagoons that concealed mythical beings. Feeding eagerly off the rain, the air built into obese rolls of clamminess that made everything smaller. It smelled like people's moist, secret crevices.

Wet children who had been caught running around the baseball field huddled together in the old hut where Susana lived with her two babies in one ragged hammock while her husband was in the big city washing dishes; it was the closest hut to the field. Rain attacked them through holes in the leafy roof. The children clasped at the posts of the doorway and watched for the rain to stop so they could go out and play again, and when they realized it was not going to stop anytime soon, they started making funny faces at each other. With a thumb into the nose or a finger tugging the corners of a mouth out, children who had played together all day, every day, all their lives were foreign to each other. First they laughed at the novelty of it, but then they became frightened.

The old man who lived next to the store that sold beer still sat outside. His son was away working in the big city and there was nobody to remind him to go inside, until the neighbour noticed him fifteen minutes into the storm. The wife he had divorced years before sat in the house she shared with her widowed sister and her children, a few doors down from his. She chuckled to herself at the thought of him sitting outside in the wet, as she knew he would be.

Rosie opened the door and looked out on the rains; it was raining stripes into the air. The light from inside the house exposed each drop of water that had left the sky and encountered them on their way to the ground.

When the rains stopped a day later, the last of the beetles had been washed away, and so had the thin, delicate bones of the birds. The ground of the hogs' pen dried under the sun into a clean, stony hardness free of dust and maggots. In the jungle outside town, brown vines dangled thickly down from the trees, like the loose threads that the bow-legged, white-haired grandmother of Rosie, Cristina, and Ismael had snipped off her sewing. Beneath them, the rain blended the freshly dug soil on top of the grave of the little girl so that nobody who passed by would have known it was there.

There were no scorpions in town or in Rosie's mind. They were entwined into a taunting mass on the outskirts of town, but they would stay there for a while.

In the stone house in the centre of town, Cristina moved restlessly in her hammock. The nameless fog that had hidden her from the world all week was beginning to subside. She slid hooks into it and hung there for as long as she could, like a rock climber, but finally she slipped down the edge and landed back into her hammock. She saw a thin line of light and went towards it. Something gave way, and there was the day and her sister next to her. The whites of Rosie's eyes were lustrous. With the very first glance, Cristina could see that her sister was irrevocably different. The acid guilt ate bitterly at her.

Cristina didn't have much to say. She put what remained of her guilt into her hand and pressed it over her heart.

—I sorry.

The tips of her short fingers were bent and crooked where they had not been before.

Like much of what people say, the gesture was more for the signer than for anyone else, but Rosie saw it for what it was and accepted it with a nod.

Neidi was the first person Rosie allowed into the house to see the recovered Cristina. She had turned away an indignant Ardrogna, whose pride was consoled by the juicy tale she had to tell about the taciturn Rosie, who Ardrogna felt had now revealed a hidden aggression.

The weakness that comes after severe illness and the

guilt transmuted in Cristina into renewed need in the edge of her that had not been eaten up, for the time when she loved Antonio and he could love her. The salty tears came out of her hot eyes and ran down her face for a long time, and they softened her insides. She felt Neidi look at her curiously and with compassion, which hurt her even more. Cristina told Neidi secrets and made sincere promises. She rested her cheek on Neidi's round shoulder but she knew Neidi could not support her infinitely. For now she gave Cristina a hole to creep through into a cradle where she could rest for some time. Neidi was witness to the injection of adrenaline and hope into Cristina's veins secret even to her.

Rosie busied herself with her hammock loom in the main room of the house as Cristina made her exorcizing confessions in her bedroom and Neidi studied the questioning fluidity that pain and fear had brought to Cristina's eyes.

The suddenly merciful days went by. After she washed the dishes from breakfast, threw the leftover tortillas to the dogs and raked the yard, Rosie swept and scrubbed every corner of the house with bleach to rid it of the cloying smell of sickness and infestation. She put the big cook-pot over the fire with some water, a chilli pepper, shredded chicken, salt, spaghetti noodles, carrots, and potatoes for a restoring stew.

Cristina was not allowed to do any housework yet. She lay in her hammock and watched her telenovelas, or walked slowly to the very end of the road and back, flanked by the open field and the shaded jungle once she got past the last house. Grit bit greedily into the yielding between her toes, but nothing else chewed at her.

Neidi came regularly to visit Cristina.

Neidi's abundant folds of flesh swallowed the disarray of others. Men that staggered on by themselves in the dark road, drunken mists coating their eyes, walked straight and calm after Neidi passed them by and laid a hand on their arms. She did not need anything in return. Her house was always tidy, but you never saw her sweeping or piles of dust out on the road in front of her house. Huge, blooming red roses lay limpid along her fence; nobody else in town had them or knew where to get them. She had never married, but she always had pesos and nobody talked about her the way they talked about Estevanya or the people in town who did not have children.

Cristina often ended up next to Neidi; at the baseball games, in church, in school when they were children.

Now, sickness and shame had peeled away a film from Cristina. She walked into the serenity of the cornfields with Neidi. The formerly congested, sniggering spaces of her life opened out. She could feel Neidi next to her, and when she looked at Neidi, she was smiling and it was voluptuous. Cristina was sheltered by being with her. She had always felt this all of the long years that she had known Neidi, but now she sank fully into the feeling as she had not and found that she wanted to stay there.

She turned the memory of her sickness over in her hands and threw it out into the cornfields. She kept the shame, but only as a reminder.

Neidi and Cristina hopped from stone to stone from there, sometimes tripping and kicking it off into the fields, but always going to find it again.

Cristina and Neidi made their way back to the road, and from the road to the house that Neidi lived in by herself, for Neidi wanted to stay in that feeling too.

Chapter Eight

Ismael walked to work along the same streets every morning and saw the same people. First the pear-shaped old woman who gave him his coffee and breakfast; and after he ate, the skinny little girl with the huge eyes selling Chiclets at the corner where the road down the mountain met the big road; the stubbly, gaunt, drunken man with the tower of sombreros on his head staggering along near the *mercado*; the man with a face like a cartoon bear and without arms and legs begging in front of the shop with the fluorescent yellow sign. They were unlike anyone Ismael had known in the village, and sometimes he drew back enough from his day-to-day-subsistence in the city to be surprised at how quickly he had become used to seeing them.

He waved to them. He wondered at the warmth with which they all returned the greeting, except for the man without arms, who nodded and smiled.

This morning, a large butterfly with peacock-feather patterns on its wings flew past him as he entered the cobblestoned square where the deaf people met. His eyes lingered on it until it flickered out of sight.

Here came the woman he dreamed about, whose startling green eyes laid all to a standstill. She was alone.

Ismael flattened himself against a wall and watched as she sat on one of the benches around the trees in the square. He saw again her brilliant eyes and her shining hair, today gathered at the nape into a bun, her full-breasted, small-waisted body under a fine black dress trimmed with red, and under it sculpted legs, crossed at the ankle. Like a little girl she tugged her feet out of their purple and green jewelled plastic sandals; the blissful air tickled the well-scrubbed soles of her feet and glided over her delicate arches. She closed her eyes and let her shoulders drop.

Ismael stayed watching her until the little hand of the clock above the store with the washing machines and re-frigerators moved, and she had not opened her eyes. There was no sign of anyone coming to join her. The skinny man with a jaw like a monkey who had watched Ismael walk through the square every morning for a week before reporting back to La Princesa stayed hidden in the crowd as he kept watch.

Ismael was late to work for the first time, and he knew he could lose his job.

Milliseconds became warm pools that submerged

Ismael, bubbles sent up to the surface. He had to find out who this woman was whom he had killed for.

He walked across the square. The seat next to her was empty and Ismael sat down there, spreading his jean-clad knees although they did not touch her. He looked down at himself; at the white T-shirt with *Wey-yano'one* printed on it in purple and his pale jeans. The *Wey-yano'one* shirt was his one souvenir from that night, other than what was in his mind. He had been wearing it at the fiesta and when he arrived at the city; all of his other clothes had been bought in the city, and he was happy to be wearing what he was that day.

But the shirt had weathered hours under the hot sun in the village and here in the city, and Cristina had scoured it insistently in her blue washbasin under the big trees. She twisted his clothes into taut rolls, chafed them against the abrasive stone till every trace of dirt and bodies was gone, unrolled them and swished the clothes in water with plenty of pale blue soap powder that stung under her fingernails and in any tiny cuts she had on her hands. Her pointed eyes searched out the underarms and collars of Ismael's work shirts and the cuffs and groins of his trousers, and she scrubbed and smashed them till they were frayed.

The woman had the tinsel of gold glittering on her

wrists and ears, and around her neck and ankles. His stained, unravelling shirt with expanding holes across the shoulders was no match for her.

Ismael remembered that night at the fiesta; the split second when he had seen himself in her and knew she saw herself in him. It stood up to all probing.

And he remembered the consequences that this woman had brought to his life and to his sisters'. He looked around at the brutish city that he lived in because of her. Questions birthed a huge litter of many-headed questions; details gave rise to wave after wave of other details. The aftershocks had not stopped making themselves felt. Shadow-lands rotated creakingly, uniting into momentarily seen tableaux of suspicion and despair before breaking apart and spinning madly until they clicked into newly tormenting juxtapositions of death and desire.

He stayed sitting next to her, waiting for her to open her eyes.

He imagined days spent shrinking into her skin as they slept, her back against his stomach. He pictured the man with the scorpion tattoos and snake eye and the other, big-bellied man bringing sudden, searing pain that would swathe his eyes, possibly for weeks on top of weeks. One by one, they would delight in popping tiny synapses in Ismael's brain out of their constraints and barbing their way into nerves he would not have known he possessed.

He shifted his weight impatiently on the bench. A soft hand with gleaming red nails descended onto his calloused one. As he looked up at her face, every detail of which he knew, the painted pink lips opened.

Never had Ismael been so humiliated to raise a finger to his ear, shake his head from side to side, again the Pac-Man hand shape by the mouth, yet again the head shake.

—Me no hear, me no speak.

He remembered having made gestures to her at the fiesta, but she must not have realized why, he thought.

She smiled and patted the air with her hand, to tell him that it was all right, she understood, she knew, as he felt she knew everything of importance about him already.

The unseen words she had spoken to him deflated, leaving dangling, helpless cords like the one at birth. Her hands tried to follow the rigorous dictates of her mouth, the mouth that must have a mind of its own and have spoken without her wanting it to.

She held out a hand to him and he took it. He remembered the feel of it from the fiesta, and again she let it lie in his own like a newborn creature. He stood when she did. Together they walked out of the square. She took deliberate, small steps. She had lowered a pair of round, black sunglasses over her eyes, so he could not see what was in them. Now that he was with her, he did not wonder who or why. Her presence rubbed that out.

They had been on one of the main roads of the city, next to a long wall painted with mournful faces posed against a cornfield that suddenly made Ismael think of the village. Now they turned down a narrow alley behind one of the buildings. Debris lay on top of the loose, uneven gravel. She had her head down, looking at the particles of stone and sand under her feet. They stopped in front of a doorway, and Ismael followed the woman up a confined flight of steps into a small, dark concrete room that reminded him of Beak-nose and her home, although this room did not feel lived in as Beak-nose's room had. The floor was thick with dust and a few cockroaches lay on their backs in it, a leg or two still wanly moving. A broken wooden chair was against one wall, and there was a stereo against another. There was a small refrigerator in one corner of the room. He could not see much else.

She took a green plastic pitcher from the refrigerator and poured from it into a glass she took from the top of the refrigerator, then handed it to him. He tasted the sweetness of citrus soda and the sharpness of tequila in it, and not the pill that the monkey man had dissolved in the pitcher earlier. She lifted the sunglasses to the top of her head, pushing back the thick hair, and smiled at him before she swayed over to the stereo and turned it on.

The nameless music thumped into him from the floor, finding itself in him, giving him the blessed gift of true anonymity in return for his recognition of it. Light plunged into the suddenly endless space above before joining into a circle over the woman's sweaty curls pressed into dark rivulets on her scalp, one winding down to rest in the bend of her plump shoulder. More light flew like moonshine from the vaporous corners of the room where she had lit a few pillar candles with Guadalupe on the glass containers.

His body remembered and trusted itself, and he snapped his fingers to lead his arm into the movement started by his leg, and the pitch and sway took him to the other side of his body, and freed his arms to touch up and around her, and his hips helped the reach of his body to expand. All was possible and near. The deepening of her dimples in the indistinct light promised him renewed happiness. He closed his eyes to discordance; to the desire for power and the vanity that he knew was in her; to exposure and indulgence; to volatility. She met him. The transience carried them with it into a reverie of ephemeral, shifting motion in flesh, shining like diamonds.

And down through it he slipped, into a heap on the cement floor, and slept deeply. Insistent, seizing fingers woke him up and brought him back into the small room, now dingy.

The woman's mouth was above him, bare of lipstick now, obstinately mumbling, demanding. The silhouettes of her invisible words landed viscerally on his skin, but Ismael did not understand how her mouth sculpted new objects from thin air, objects that she expected him to see. He did not see them, he could not hold them, he did not believe in them. People in the village did not need these things.

She shook him and moved her mouth again and again. He turned his head from side to side, and she left. He was alone in the dirty room. When he tried the single, heavy door, it was securely locked.

He looked through the metal shutters in the tiny slit high up in the front wall at the far off mountains crowned in white fog, or down at the floor where ants marched in a line to the door. The syrupy light was sucked into the parched room only to disappear.

Even without anyone else there, the antagonism spanned from one end of the room to the other.

If he had felt powerless in the city from the start, Ismael was now forsaken. Yet when he thought about what he would have done differently, he did not know that either.

He sat on the broken chair, wishing for insight or illumination. The demarcations of this new life had finally landed only to shift abruptly, and they forced out the relative ease he had found so recently.

The questions that had left him upon seeing her again and the apparitions he had been vigilantly keeping at bay came back, and they multiplied fast and furious. He understood now that she was a completely different person than he had first thought she was. At the very least, she was working for other people; possibly they were working for her. He did not understand what use he was to her, and why he was not dead.

Seeing that this was what had separated him from his sisters and from the village and his language, he was sickened.

Yet when he remembered dancing with her at the fiesta and earlier that day in the room, his insides quickened.

Could that look in her eyes have been false? He could not believe it entirely, both out of sentimental longing and hard reason. It must be what kept him alive, because there was nothing else. He knew what she had freed inside of him was not false.

Still, he could easily die here in this room now.

He took his feet out of their rubber sandals and brushed them over the dust of the floor. It made him think of how she had taken her feet out of the sandals in the square. She had not seemed surprised to see him.

Black specks clouded in front of the window. Ismael jumped up and down below it, trying to see if he could reach into it; but it was a tiny slit far above him.

A large beetle rushed across the floor and under a wall, its antennae wavering. Segmented brown exoskeleton jerked out of a corner, and Ismael saw that it was a small scorpion. Seeing it, fury filled him for the first time since the night of the fiesta when everything had changed. It was a damned ugly creature, it looked as noxious as it was. It seemed to embody the elemental discontent and distur-bance that had entered him the night of the fiesta and that he now felt had always been a part of him, and of the colossal, hurt animal of the world.

Like a steel-toothed trap his hands annihilated it, and through his crushing fingers brown stink dripped. There. He had taken care of it, as neatly and finally as he had taken care of the lizards and birds he had killed with his slingshot as a boy in the village.

It had been a long time since Ismael had felt entirely satisfied with himself. He got up from the broken chair and straightened his shoulders; he smoothed his curly hair with his fingers and ran a pinky finger, wetted in his mouth, across each eyebrow. Opening the refrigerator, he saw a bottle of clear liquid. Unscrewing the cap, he smelled it; it was water. He drank greedily, swishing it through his mouth, dislodging stale flavours and lingering impressions. The room breathed bigger and Ismael felt easier.

He sat back down on the chair, rearranging his body, and concentrated on the stained grey wall in front of him. The blotches were more fluid than any tools to explain what he felt. They were there in front of his eyes, so he could believe in them completely.

Soon after the light outside the slit darkened into the obscure, secret night, the door opened and the man with the snake eye and scorpion tattoos entered, feet turned outwards in his pointed orange snakeskin boots. He was alone. His lips hung lax off the brassy teeth. He crossed the room and knelt in front of Ismael before he opened his mouth; the woman must have told him that Ismael was deaf. But when he opened his overhung jaw, sprinkled with rhinestone inserts in gold teeth next to the lacklustre yellow ones, the intangible words that came out with a jeer felt to Ismael like the crudely drawn flames shooting out of an arcade game. They poured down hard onto Ismael.

Ismael turned his palms inwards; an upright flattened palm against another upright flattened palm, in the same gesture people used when they prayed, and which Ismael punctuated with a head nod. Please. His index finger went to his mouth to say that it would not ever open, nothing would be let loose from it. Then both hands became upright flattened palms again, and their backs went to lie flat by each of his shoulders to indicate the end of the short negotiation. That was the only thing Ismael felt he had to offer to the man and his friends: his silence, a smooth ball to be manipulated however that snake eye wished.

The man did not want it, did not even consider it. Contempt came into the one brown eye so that it matched the expression in the unchanging snake eye. His hammy hands shoved Ismael hard against the wall before one went into a back pocket of his tight jeans and drew out a photograph that he showed to Ismael. He recognized the broad face and suspicious, small eyes of the man that he had killed.

Ismael had not provoked the dead man intentionally; he had chased after Ismael, thrust him into the corner of the cantina, and it had only been then that Ismael drew his gun. Before that, the woman danced with him by her own choice. Again, Ismael tried to understand how he had gotten here.

The door opened and the woman re-entered, slamming the metal door hard behind her in warning. Ismael watched her speak phantasmagoria to the man, taking the man with her into them, laughing at what was around them. She did not look at Ismael. Something was thrashing about in both of them and forcing Ismael down. He wanted to take a sharp pin to her words, to pop them flat and make them fall limp onto the floor. What would these people do if they were stuck in the clear matter of silence with him? They would struggle furiously and sink deeper and deeper into the quicksand. He would throw ropes and poles down to them, but they would be refused.

The man turned away and walked into a corner of the room, to fire another barrage of shells and grenades from his mouth into a small silver phone he took from his pocket.

For the first time since the fiesta, she looked directly at Ismael. The enveloping narcissism fell away from her eyes and Ismael saw what he had seen then. Everything was intact and present. Regret came to Ismael like a dark cloud into a sunny day, feeling inevitable within a few seconds, and he saw it in her too.

The man finished on the phone and turned to them. On cue, the curtain came back down onto the stage of the woman's eyes, but not before the man had seen the vibrancy of the players bowing and departing. The glaring orange cinders of anger flew into the snake-eyed man, struck a charge, and lit it as easy and sure as a match to a puddle of gas. Spleen distended his stomach. It ballooned and the balloon popped. The gas puffed up his cheeks; some of it formed itself into shapes around his bumpy red tongue and made his lips vibrate fast and funny when it escaped his mouth, wrapped around words intended for the green-eyed woman. Gobbets of spittle flew across the room and landed on Ismael.

Ismael knew the blight had come again to scorch him and toughen his skin.

But his skin was still not too tough to be pierced.

Ismael saw the metallic glint of the knife in the man's hand. He saw the man look to the woman for permission. She gave it with a nod, as she must have to the man Ismael had killed at the fiesta. This time, Ismael saw the tyranny in her eyes flare up in response to his waking vulnerability.

The next thing he knew was the knife in him, blood answering. He saw the spatters of brown-red from his chest descend onto his dusty feet. He looked through the red at the woman before it came down into his chest again; then the knife lay beside him on the dirty floor, next to a pool of the blood that uncoiled like a centipede from Ismael. Some of it entered his mouth, and the nutty warmth tasted richer than any food. Its metal smell came into Ismael's nostrils.

As he lay curled up on the floor, he saw the orange snakeskin boots whacking stolidly against the floor on their way to the door, then the jewelled sandals followed, lightly. Through his pain, he looked up at her, but she had the sunglasses down over her eyes as she left the room. He knew the only place he would ever see her again was in his mind.

He stayed there, curled up on the floor, through another change of light dimly sensed via the slit high up on the wall. He felt the judders of his body and the rutted hum inside him that came from his screams. His hands clenched in the same way that babies grasp when they suckle milk. His legs straightened and then they let go.

As the pong of rancid flesh filled the room, he braced himself against the wall and got to his feet. The last of the water from the bottle in the refrigerator returned his mouth to him. He felt his way along the wall to the door. It was unlocked. He sat on the landing and lowered himself to sit on the next step and the next, one by one all the way to the bottom, like a toddler.

On the walk back to the village from the cantina after the fiesta, Ismael had thought of his grandfather on his long, futile walk back to the village after being shot by his wife. Now Ismael felt he was his grandfather. He prayed and he thought of Rosie and Cristina. All else disappeared into the creases of time and suffering.

Unusually, there were no birds in the cerulean sky; when Ismael's eyes ranged out looking for them, he found the birds in a blur above the church. Their abundance entered him and stroked his sore eyeballs.

He staggered along the stony alley, tripping into a rut to land heavily onto a rusty piece of barbed wire that scratched his cheek. Red came out from under the hand Ismael held up to his face and trickled leisurely down until it met the red coming out from his chest.

Turning briefly into a doorway, Ismael gingerly rolled up his white *Wey-yano'one* T-shirt, now covered with dried blood. He examined the parallel cuts in his chest. They were between his nipples, and they stretched about an inch each. The ragged flaps of skin that lay open revealed the raw meat of him. He was relieved to see that for all the blood and the concentration of his entire body onto these two throbbing slits, they did not run horribly deep; but his heart was etched.

Army trucks rolled slowly down the street next to him, navy blue suited policemen staring out with vacant hostility from behind dark sunglasses. Ismael startled, bent over hastily to conceal his chest, whipped towards the wall. Why did he feel that he was a fugitive? He felt more of one now than he had after killing the man. But he had known who he was then.

The last of the trucks passed. He could not afford a doctor and he did not want to turn to anyone for help. He felt in his pocket; he had been paid for a week of work the day before and there was a roll of bills there. Holding one arm to his chest, he held the other arm aloft and looked for a taxi. He had never flagged one down before. He hoped they would think he had been in a fight; it was not a rare thing, and he did not think he appeared to be drunk.

Several passed by before one swerved to the kerb for Ismael. He pointed the way to the big road, and from there to the road up the mountain. The driver did not ask anything, not even with the purplish, prunelike eyes Ismael saw reflected in the rear-view mirror.

He took each step up to his hammock on his hands and knees, the same way he had taken the steps down from the room, and slept for a while on the top step before he hauled himself up the last few. There was a bottle of aspirin in one of his plastic bags. He swallowed down four of the chalky tablets, dampened a rag with bottled water, and wiped the blood from his skin. Then he slept.

The same fog that had recently left Cristina came down on him, and the occurrence of Cristina was there in the fog, beyond a viscous miasma. He felt the scorpion beneath everything, as she had; but it was different for him, because he had not let it loose and he had conquered it in that small room the green-eyed woman led him into, before the knife came down. Other, sated influences drifted past in the fog. The amorphous illness grasped his limbs tight. He came to the edge of a cavity and peered cautiously into it. It was a deep hole of deadened black. Things came tumbling down, he could not find a foothold; he floated deliriously in agony; then he came to a place where it stayed solid for some time. Filaments of silvery spiderweb shimmered for a moment in front of his eyes and they were a consecration. It was only then that he started trembling.

He lay there for a long while.

Ismael awoke to the thought that he was not his grandfather after all. He remembered what the priest said: that he, Rosie and Cristina had been born deaf because of what their grandmother had done. In the village, he had never been able to understand completely what the priest meant. Now that the blood came again, he understood more than the priest himself had, even as he realized that these words had taken him to this place he was in now. But Ismael did not think it was a curse. It was a blessing. One that slipped like a rope around their necks; but there was a rope around everyone's necks, and Ismael now felt that, as much as words and confession could have saved his grandmother, his own sign language forced him back down firm onto the ground. The green-eyed woman was still hovering, fastened to the puffed up balloons of her words, and she would always live in her shadow-land.

When he arose from the hammock, he slowly ate a packet of stale vanilla sandwich biscuits that had been in one of the plastic bags, carefully preventing crumbs falling into the wounds on his chest, already coagulating.

Then he washed the *Wey-yano'one* T-shirt in a pail of water he had drawn from a neighbour's reservoir to wet and tamp down the dirt around the hammock on what now seemed a long ago day. The rusty stains on the shirt leached out and became fragile swirls. It took some heavy-duty scrubbing with a bar of soap, but finally the cloth was a semblance of white again, with two new holes through the front. He wrung it out as hard as he could. The wrinkles still showed in the cloth when he put it on the line strung from one pole of his shelter to a nearby tree.

He would keep the shirt always, as a souvenir. The shirt, and the scars. They would brand him like a cow.

The little girl in the turquoise house that was the nearest one to Ismael often came to wave and grin saucily at him in the hours just before twilight. Now her impish face rose behind the poles of the lean-to, and she poked her tongue out. Instead of raising his head from the hammock to stick his tongue back at the girl to prompt her into scrunching her eyes in merriment and leaping up on a tree to corkscrew into the clandestine leaves, Ismael made a circle with one of his hands, tore away a paper lid, poured into it with his other hand, drew a noodle from it with the pincers of his thumb and forefinger, dangled it above his open mouth before dropping it in, and took a few pesos from his hand to put into hers; enough for the noodles and a treat for herself.

Now she brought him containers of instant noodles with hot water poured in every evening, and he thought of Rosie who loved them.

Infection had not set in as he had been afraid it would, and Ismael prescribed more rest and more aspirin for himself.

Every morning, the laughing wind woke him and each time, more life returned to Ismael.

Before another week went by, he realized the substance of his days was no longer flaking off. Ismael started to believe that the green-eyed woman had ceased to taint the cadence of his life.

He needed to see other people, to enter into everyday life and bustle to prove it to himself. Taking the gauze that the little girl had brought him, he taped it in layers over the wounds, then put his bare feet onto the hot, dry dirt of the ground. A few aching steps down the flight of stairs that had felt insurmountable, and he stood by the side of the road until a corroded black pickup truck stopped and the driver snapped a forefinger forward to see if he wanted a ride. He did.

He did not know where the truck was going, but down the road, away from the confusion of the scrub at the top of the mountain and towards the comparative order of the city, felt right to Ismael.

He was thankful that he was able to get into the cab with the driver and not ride in the back; he was not sure if the still healing but inflamed cuts could have taken the jolts of the back, even as he longed for the air blowing freely over his skin and through his hair after the days lying in motionless, muggy air.

When the brawny, curly-haired driver glanced at him briefly and nodded, Ismael felt less of a fugitive than he had since the fiesta. He did not think it was completely over, but the tension of the anticipation that had hung in the air even more heavily than the heat had lessened.

The springs of the broken seat poked up into his thigh through his jeans, and he rolled open the window to the air, invigorated by the speed of the truck engine. Down the mountain, passing the stores and dwellings that he had seen so many times before and was surprisingly happy to see again now. Through the central square with its overhanging shade trees. Ismael gazed at the Maya sitting cross-legged along it, selling sweets, and new energy rose. His lips pursed around the developing stone of his resolve.

The truck stopped in front of the *mercado*. Ismael felt deflated to be back at the site of much that had passed, but he thanked the driver with a hand held in the air and got out.

Entering the *mercado* by a congested corridor shingled with bootleg DVDs in plastic sleeves, Ismael turned towards the corner where Beak-nose squeezed orange juice, then stopped and went in another direction. He thought of the feel of her lean body with its soft stomach when he turned to her in the middle of the night; of the star earrings, the exact purplish pink of the papery flowers that vined all over the city, which had brought him to the deaf here in the city.

The wound and sickness still drummed kinetically on him, and Ismael wished for Beak-nose in a way that he had never wished for his former wife, Flat-face; but he grasped onto the wishing as tightly as he had onto the scorpion, and killed it with as much finality.

He was relieved that the green-eyed woman did not enter into him. Possibly he was truly rid of her. The thought itself was dangerous, so he did away with it also.

He walked further into the market, meandering from the rabbit's feet and beads to the coffee and honey. Women with woven plastic bags heavy with the week's shopping over their arms, leaves and sprigs topping all off, and men with wet eyes under the wide white brims of their hats passed him. The wounds did not pulse any more than they had, and the thought of the green-eyed woman was still dead. He would mend eventually.

Ismael would find yet another job, he thought, but this

time he would be able to stay with it. He would go back to the square and the deaf people every week; perhaps he would even go to buy orange juice from Beak-nose, but once a few months had passed.

He thought of the village and of trying to go back, but he would not risk putting any of them into danger by his presence, and Jose's verdict retained its weight. Not as much commotion pushed up against Rosie and Cristina when they came into his mind; they had more room now, and he could look at them for much longer and from more angles. Maybe the turmoil would return once he was completely recovered.

He smelled cooking food. He was famished. He had not eaten anything except instant soup for more than a week. He felt in his pocket for money and sat down in front of a woman with pink rhinestones butterflying across her hair. The man next to him was eating *posole* and drinking a Coca-Cola, and Ismael pointed to them and then to himself to indicate that he wanted the same. The flavours filled his mouth completely. He took a tortilla from the hot stack wrapped in an embroidered cloth that the woman had set down in front of him and moved it around the plate, wetting it with grease and folding it into a tube that he put into his mouth, sucking the warm, oily gravies deep into his marrow.

Ismael closed his eyes and watched the back of his eyelids glow. One hefty hand fell slowly down the slope of his belly to land crumpled on the bench he was sitting on. Then it was the turn of each finger to open flat into relaxation.

A human hand bore down on his back. Ismael turned around. It did not feel like the green-eyed woman's touch, nor the touch of either of her men.

It was Jose from the village. Jose, the only person who knew why he had left, who had told him to leave. His name sign was forefinger into cheek, for his dimples, and today they went further into his cheek than Ismael had ever seen them go.

Jose brought his beautiful hands up and from them flowed the purest, most magical medicine Ismael could have hoped for. It slid down to gently soak the disturbance in his chest.

—Ismael-strong, Ismael-strong! Thumb up, you OK? Hand reach far back behind . . . Long long time! Long long time! Me eyes-open-big much surprise see you, much much happy see you.

Ismael had forgotten the naughtiness in Jose's bird-bright eyes and the clown's grin that seemed too alive for his heavy, meaty body, one that seemed like it should be slumped in a chair, shirt covered with orange slicks of grease.

His T-shirt was kept rolled up above his corpulent brown belly, and the grey pants and black snakeskin belt he always wore rode low below his hip bones. Remembering, Ismael giggled wildly, a little boy again. His arms went up behind Jose's squat body and around him as tightly as they could. The cuts carved into his chest screeched, but Ismael did not feel them.

Then Jose sat next to Ismael at the counter and told the woman to bring beer as they talked for hours. Jose told Ismael that Cristina had run away with the man in the tiger kerchief, and the village had worried about Rosie, but she had pulled through strong. That Rosie had soothed Cristina upon her return, and that Cristina had been ill after tearing so roughly at her sister. Jose did not tell Ismael that much of the time now Cristina was with Neidi, because he did not know. Estevanya was now pregnant and married to the schoolmaster from Nayarit, and their house was the tidiest in the village.

Ismael told Jose everything that had happened to him in the city. His hands whittled the outlines of the ghostly terrain he had inhabited. In telling Jose, Ismael knew he was helping to rid himself of it. He told of the green-eyed woman and her men; of Beak-nose and the deaf people; of the jobs and his red hammock on the mountain.

Most of all, he told of what had been boiling inside him

and spilling out. His hands surged up from his stomach and flew luridly around him before they ruthlessly entered him again, and rotated back outside. He drew up his shirt to show Jose the bandages, and the bandages to show the cuts writhing like leeches underneath.

—Them them them point-there in home, them Pac-Man handshape talk talk me still? After eye-like-growing-plant woman finish stab me, you think me still finger-shake no-no back home? Me need stay here city on on on into hand-ahead-of-body future?

As he said it, the possibility of going home became palpable for Ismael; the smell of the cornfields at harvesting, the flavour of Cristina's lentil and pumpkin seed empanadas, the wooden stool by the fire in the morning. The coarse, freckled skin on his sisters' arms. The particular pattern that the hammocks Rosie made imprinted in his back in the night.

Before he had left, Ismael had been spoon-feeding an emaciated grey kitten that lay against the concrete block of the kitchen fire for three days, ashes blistering its thin fur, after an attack by Estevanya's bully of an orange cat. It had finally started to fatten up when the older cat leapt onto it with both incisors bared. Rosie would not let Ismael and Cristina bury it, or lay it under the rubber mat in the yard. Its chest still expanded sporadically, and the day of the fiesta it rose from the dead and tottered over to lap from Rosie's morning bowl of powdered milk. Was it still alive? Ismael wondered, for the first time since he had last seen it.

He seized his hands into fists and felt his nails press into his palms as he waited for Jose's answer. His nails were overgrown and had dirt and blood under them, he suddenly realized.

Jose questioned Ismael again on exactly what had happened with the green-eyed woman, both at the fiesta and in the city, and on all the times he had seen her and her men.

He would go and talk to some friends who understood the narcos, he told Ismael. They had to be completely sure. He would be here in the city a week longer, working construction. Jose was staying with cousins in a large-roomed, fuchsia-walled house nearby, with a mint-green tiled kitchen where chicken and rice were always cooking in big pots on the stove. Did Ismael want to stay there too?

He did, and he followed Jose there after they finished the next beer. Jose's cousin Ignacio came out to take them into his burly arms, then his plain, worn-down wife into her brittle ones, and their little girl painted Ismael's toenails with a bottle of bright pink nail polish.

Against the side wall of the house sprawled a child-sized rag doll, red-stitched mouth tittering blindly under black button eyes. It had been dumped from a passing truck. Ismael shrugged one shoulder in replication and let his arms hang wobbly, his head lying forward on his chest. At the sight of Ismael embodying a helpless being, gales of laughter came to the little girl, and it only took a look towards the doll and a lift of the clavicle to bring them out again and again.

Ismael liked seeing her laugh, but he thought to himself that the imitation was so good because he was now the rag doll.

There was room for one more man on the construction site, but Ismael's cuts were still healing. He lay in the hammock Ignacio strung up for him in the house, watching wrestlers crash into each other on the radiant electric box and the neighbours coming into the house to ask for an egg, a beer, to buy some of the pork tamales that Ignacio's wife sold in front of the house. The dog of the house was white with brown spots and an under-bite that made him look mean when he was just silly. He rubbed his back against Ismael's weight rounding out the bottom of the hammock. The woven rope chafed roughly against the dog's itchy spots. Under the hammock the dog went, bumping Ismael up and down to scratch out the fleas. A few twitches and shakes under Ismael, and he was out on the other side and down the other way again.

Just below the ceiling, a framed photograph of Ignacio's macho brother Santiago glowered down; he spent long nights in the Jaguar strip club with others from the cartel.

Ismael had not passed days on end in the daily commotion of people going around their lives next to one another since he left the village, and he learnt it again, the way they moved past the others in the house, the way they met eyes and indicated whether they were now going somewhere else or if they could stop. It seemed difficult and complex to Ismael now where it never had in the village, before the scars. Would it feel different being in his house in the village with Rosie and Cristina? he suddenly wondered. The repairing wounds on his chest tensed into warning.

Jose came home late at night, after a few beers with the men from the construction job, and always Ismael put all into his hands for him and saw the true contour and line of things, as he had not when they were contained in him.

One day Jose told Ismael that he now knew who to ask if it was safe for Ismael to return to the village. A few days later, Jose visited the jail, where men lay on concrete platforms in the unlighted drunk tank. Words were scrawled in black on the walls, words that had loitered within the men, pressing for a way out.

The man Jose was there to see had been curled up in the corner of the tank, bloodshot eyes swollen with alcohol. He looked back and forth, back and forth like an antagonistic rooster; the room drank it up and spells of fighting spurted out into the nothingness that lay heavily on the men.

The man had worked with La Princesa for years. Jose explained all he knew to him, and in return for a few pesos, the man told Jose that if the green-eyed woman had Ismael in a room and did not make sure that he was dead, she and her men did not intend to kill him, had carried out what they meant to, and would not be looking for him. It was safe for Ismael to go where he wished.

Ismael's desire to know more about her rushed to his head and made him dizzy. It was stronger than ever. But every time he had taken a turn in the labyrinth that she was at the centre of, something had sprung up and sunk its teeth into him. He did not ask any more; did not think any more. Beneath that lay a certainty that she was someone who all of Mexico would know one day.

For the second time in his life, Ismael took a taxi up to his red hammock in the mountains. This time, the taxi waited as Ismael took down his hammock and gave it to the little girl who had brought him soup; he gathered up the plastic bags from the posts and stood looking down on the jungle roof one last time. The stingers of the pointed thoughts that the heat brought retracted as the day abated, and with the temperate breezes of early evening came wistfulness. The luxuriant green of the trees beneath him engulfed Ismael in the remembering of the troubles and the seraphs that had come to him here. He hoped that some of the angels would travel with him. He felt that what had happened had not sullied his newfound potential to feel the divine.

He loaded the bags into the taxi and showed the driver the piece of paper Ignacio had given him with the address of the fuchsia-walled house.

A few days later, after Jose finished his construction job, he and Ismael loaded more plastic bags with candy from a nearby store, for the village children. They scooped black beans and white rice from burlap sacks into smaller bags and bought jars and jars of lard. Ismael studied the wares for sale in the city carefully before he bought a dark pink knitted shawl for Rosie and bright green-blue lizardskin high heels for Cristina with the last of his money. Then they hoisted all the packages to the bus station where they sat surrounded by weary Maya waiting for the chariot that would return them to their villages.

Soon Ismael was on his way back to his village, to the language he understood and the people who signed it, to live with his sisters Rosie and Cristina in the concrete-block house that he had built onto the lean-to that once belonged to their parents.

He had two thick, raised red welts on his chest that had not been there when he left the village. But the most significant new disfigurement could not be seen by anyone, not even by Ismael himself.

Chapter Nine

Rosie and Cristina did not work side by side now. Cristina wanted to stay at home and cook or sweep and mop and tamp down the dirt of the courtyard, and she told Rosie to cut firewood, or stockpile food for the cows. Rosie fixed the irrigation system she had rigged up on their vegetable garden and patched holes in the fence around it. Sometimes she went to Juan-Deafy's to tear palm leaves down from the low trees at the back of his land. She ran the leaves over the top of a flaming branch to harden them before cutting them down for tamale wrappers.

Today, she was in the field. There was a promising clump of bushes in one corner, past a low-growing shrub covered in tiny violet flowers. She started her pile of cow fodder with the bushes, and then ranged out further into the meadow. The mound grew higher. She chopped for a long while at a veiny root that was thin but stubborn. The very last sinews refused to give way, and she bent over to wrest it free. It looked like a rodent's tail, and it was as sly and dogged as a rat. Rosie wrested it back and forth, not letting it escape from her grasp, until it relented and she added it to her springy heap of branches and stalks. The rope went around it and was knotted tightly over. With a heave, she propped the bunch up on the shelf of her bottom and lowered the rope onto her forehead.

Rosie followed the narrow, long path as it turned crookedly through the woods, coming back to itself and slithering past a scraggy old tree. Looking at the tree, she realized it was the spiky one covered with prickly thorns, and opposite it would be the strong one that reassured. She stopped exactly between the two trees and studied them. She wondered if one sensed the other. They grew in the hot sun on either side of the path, one closer to the jungle and one closer to the village.

Rosie could touch both at the same time if she stretched out her arms. She tapped a finger on the tip of a thorn and she caressed the trunk of the big tree.

The thorn she now rubbed her finger over felt like a sharp, annihilating knife, even with her other hand on the primeval bulk of the strong tree.

She drew her hand back from the thorn, placed her burden onto the ground, and leant against the big tree. Again, she felt something in her reply tenaciously to the big tree, but the thorn pricked and pierced a serrated hole that did not completely repair, as it would have before Cristina reached into her.

She knew the scorpions were still nearby, a great crackling mass climbing upwards in twitchy agitation.

Rosie sat by the big tree for as long as she could. She remembered her brother Ismael, but the thought did not placate her.

Then she continued along the path till it met the road. The stack of fodder drew the thin, coarse rope tightly against her forehead, where it made a deep abrasion like a crown of thorns. She reached their house, set her load down, and sat in the dim peacefulness of the front room, lifting her head when Cristiano from next door emerged momentarily from beneath her elbow, grinning with a child's mischief. He clung to her for a few minutes, but when other children passed in front of the house, he drew away from her and ran home.

Lupita across the street paid Rosie to wash her clothes because she had too much on her hands looking after her two granddaughters while their mother worked as a maid in the big city during the week. Nobody knew where their father was. The oldest child bit her grandmother all over, leaving red marks behind. She missed her mother.

Now Lupita was outside her house, sitting on her purple rubber chair with the two girls playing in the dirt near her. Rosie could see her through the trees at the front of her property.

The twisted posts of Lupita's fence leant backwards, pushing a tree sideways, and the stray threads from Lupita's hammock loom lay scattered near the gate into her yard. In front of Lupita's house, a blue string made a half circle around a burnt remote control plane, the left wing missing. By Sunday, the oldest granddaughter had broken the toys that her mother brought back every Friday from the city. Next to the plane was withered orange peel.

When Rosie lifted herself off the steps and walked to the store to get soda, orange squares of cheese and flour tortillas for the evening meal, her skinny calves taking careful steps under the gentle swaying of her pink skirt, the spotlights that the village had bought a few years back were on. The small basketball court was lit as if it were a professional sports stadium. The weaker lights in front of the nearby store were more hospitable, and that was where the men sat with their beer, looking somewhere that their wives, their children, their sisters and brothers, their parents, their lovers, their best friends had no idea about.

Outside of the circles of light, the night was unusually black. There were no stars in the sky to dive through, and the indistinct shapes of the houses and trucks parked outside sank into the dark and were consumed.

Rosie did not know if she should cook for Cristina as well. Some nights Cristina was home, most nights she was not. Rosie always waited until the metal door closed after Cristina and the room was dark again before she opened her eyes, and she faced the wall and not Cristina's hammock when her sister came back into the house.

Tonight, when she opened the door with the bag of food in her hand and a wide panel of light was inserted into the dusky rooms, she saw that nobody was in the house.

The man with the tiger kerchief and Cristina's illness had been interruptions in the sisters' days, but Neidi was something different. Neidi tied Cristina down in the same way that Ismael had; in a way that Rosie knew she could not. Rosie let her sister's deceits dissipate in the air in front of her unblinking eyes, and Ismael and Neidi did not.

Rosie longed for more division from the world, for a semblance of influence, but always it was a fantasy.

Things would go on this way; neither she nor Cristina were able to say anything about what really went on inside their chests, and Cristina would spend more and more time with Neidi.

A claw clenched tightly onto Rosie's heart, and when it joined the one that had been there since Ismael left, the two claws encompassed her heart and the fear shook itself out in her veins like a wet dog and deposited its larva all through her body.

She was without comprehension or compression into likelihoods and risks.

She was not afraid of being alone, but she had always lived together with her parents or one or both of her siblings in this house. The only thing she remembered of life without Cristina was an image, streaky with childhood light, of an old red hammock sagging with the weight of Ismael lying next to her, both of them open-eyed in the darkness of the room as they waited to meet the new baby.

She went behind the chicken hutches, sat on the pile of cement blocks Ismael had piled up there, feeling the wire of the hutches cut reassuringly into her back, and wondered if she could just stay there. Or start walking now, and keep walking, out and out, on a road which would become narrow, barely wide enough for one person. All would not come apart out there; she could follow the edge of the abyss and keep going, in a somewhat familiar but anonymous new world.

The dark permeated, and for the first time in her life, Rosie felt decay rushing onto her.

What had happened to their grandmother had always been in the air around the siblings, but Rosie had always felt that it would stay there. That the push and pull, tug and thrust between her brother and sister, with Rosie in the middle keeping the peace, would keep everything in balance always. Ismael had given in to the curse as Rosie had not thought he would, and now it was lopsided.

She took off her dress and sat on the balls of her feet in her white half-slip with the hand-embroidered lace across the bottom. Her breasts hung down her chest, crumpled and empty.

The spiky tree back in the field entered her dreams that night, its trunk crawling with scorpions convulsing with venom, and she forgot about the existence of the other tree until she woke. In the morning, the hammock next to hers was still empty and those three-pointed thorns prickled and punctured her mind.

She could not quiet them. She was perilously alone and dehydrated.

Cupped hand, other cupped hand, half-ball two, spin spin different direction, stop fingers stuck, hands up make ghost not know what hands on chest feel jumble, head-turn. Hand still, other hand below pop pop mix mix alive there, much fall red there. Again half-ball spin spin different directions it not stop it not stop it never stop now not know what to do since long time not know no more me Rosie-old not know no more me Rosie-old tired me Rosie-old tired tired tired.

—Finger across neck, tongue out-mouth, hands down by legs.

That was the sign for death.

Her lover was on the other side of the basketball court in the middle of a crowd filled with rages and uncontainable urges, but Cristina knew exactly where she was, and Neidi knew where Cristina was.

Cristina had hoped and hoped for something to find and redeem her, and it had. There was no need for them to become accustomed to a shared tempo. It was there. Neidi quietly understood all of Cristina's sparky, ragged bits and how they entered the world. The tedium no longer irritated her so quickly. Her hand left off fiddling with the stolen plastic dog and her tongue left off poking repeatedly in and out of the wet hole in the back of her mouth. The domineering vim had evaporated. Her body did not sag with guilt and anxiety any longer.

Since Ismael had left, and for most of the time even before, Cristina's unnamed anxiety had smashed her viscera into smithereens, so that her arms and hands could not compress them into expression. They could only quake in manifestation of what was inside her, like the movements of the lava at the mouth of a volcano. She had been unable to talk about her inner workings; she only talked about the minutiae of what lay around her.

Now when Cristina looked out at the pale swells of the cornfields that surrounded her, they were mirrored inside her entirety and she put them into her hands and arms. The details that had occupied her for most of her life did not seem significant. She made her fingers into the heads of the plants as they bristled up from the ground in row after row, then she changed the perspective of the scene and her palms became the mild, golden waves of the fields as they followed the earth, on and on in all directions.

The land was in much of the language and the language was now fully embedded in Cristina.

She did not talk to Ardrogna any longer, nor did she loiter outside the tortilleria with the other women or smoke in Ismael's room. The talk that had coated her so thickly eroded; what she had thought of as her emotions fell away, and entities that more closely matched the landscape around her came through.

She was more easily penetrated in this new state, but she did not draw the protective cloak of talk around herself again, for Neidi was next to her, enveloping her.

She was surprised at the subsiding of her desire to have Ismael there with them in the village. She was glad that he was far away, with his certainty that he knew what was best for her. She did not stop hoping that he was all right, but since her sickness, she did not fear the scorpion tattooed man with the same intensity, nor the green-eyed woman. Something else was coming into her that replaced all of the fear, pathos, and apprehension. It came and it made her feel. There were other bodies near her own, Cristina realized. Now when Cristina looked at the plants growing up the side of her house and sap dripped from the plant as branch fell to ground, she felt it as she had not, and the reason and the story ceased to be of importance to her. Instead, a regular pulse rocked high and wide in her, pushing everything else out.

It always led her to Neidi.

At first, Cristina went to sleep at the same time as unknowing Rosie every night. Once she was certain her sister was lost in sleep, she disturbed the night as she opened the door and walked out in her newly bought pale pink lacy nightgown, bought from the man who came to the village every few months to lay out new garments in the back of his truck. It was a strangely girlish garment for her. She pushed one foot and then the other into a pair of Ismael's work boots and straightened Ismael's bicycle from the fence it had been leaning on. Cristina rode along the potholed road towards the jungle, the air rushing through the fine weave of the nightie to land cold on her skin, her feet clammy in the sucking rubber of the too-big boots. The tyre of the bicycle swerved on the ups and downs, and her body met the upsurges with nothing less than glee. She closed her eyes to feel the unsullied night on her face and almost missed the tall palm tree that marked the turn-off onto the small path that led to the dormant volcano. Neidi was waiting for her in a lean-to near it.

The first time, they hacked their way through the leaves and trees with a wood-handled machete Neidi kept sheathed on a rope around her waist. Sweat collected in the corners of their bodies. Cristina kept one hand in Neidi's as they went further into the jungle, and Neidi was careful not to let her knife rebound into Cristina's body as she angled the blade first left and then right, cutting away the snaked-together vines that blocked their way to the lean-to that was now sanctuary to Cristina's homeless desire.

The village could not know about them.

Cristina flew when she was with Neidi, and when she came back into the village and her life.

Now, Cristina did not wait until Rosie had gone to sleep before she left. Love made her forget. She failed to see Rosie, as she had not when she was with the tiger-kerchief man.

Cristina only knew that the more she could be alone, the more chance there was of seeing Neidi; that if Rosie was working in the fields and Cristina was home cooking, Neidi could come to see her for a few minutes.

In the late morning, while Rosie was out in the fields, Cristina made a rich pork, tomato and black bean stew flavoured with garlic, onion, lime, salt, and chilli and pounded rounds of tortilla dough in one palm to fry on the skillet above the fire before adding them to the stack on the table. The round red tomatoes gave way under Cristina's knife and she saw hard white seeds in yellowish liquid globules. The crystalline salt dissolved in the golden oil. The knife chinked against the wooden cutting board as she chopped the small red chillies. And Neidi's round, balmy arms came around her waist and turned Cristina towards contentment.

Later, she sat across the table from Rosie as Rosie dipped tortillas into the stew, made shells to hold beans and greasy bits of pork, made sure she got all of the juices from her bowl. Cristina's new susceptibility erected a screen between her and Rosie; she was a child wanting to take in the world and neglecting what was closest.

Just a few weeks before, Rosie and Cristina had not seen the division between them, and now they were alienated.

That evening, as Cristina put what was left of the stew back onto the cooking fire for their supper, her eyes were fixed on the red flowers growing from the tree behind Rosie. Yellow rounds of pollen clustered along the stamens of the flowers, and the wind rustled the tree. As soon as

Rosie finished eating, Cristina would say she needed to go to the store to buy more dish soap to wash up for the night. She would take the circle road that went past the pink house where Neidi lived, and maybe Neidi would be out front feeding table scraps to the dogs.

As soon as it got dark, she would be on her bicycle, her way lit by the blazing gem of the moon.

Rosie sat with outspread legs on her low wooden stool in the dirt, her eyes on Cristina as she slowly ate the stew. Her lip stayed up after she spooned more pork into her mouth, above her crooked yellowish teeth with a gap between the two front ones. She shoved a cold, hardening corn tortilla into her mouth, in the back where it wouldn't catch on her crumbling teeth.

The unbridgeable split between the sisters expanded unhurriedly into the hush. There was nothing that could change it.

Chapter Ten

The lights on the bus had been turned out for the night and sleep shrouded the fatigued men and women, their skin slack and tinged with yellow from the hours, days, and weeks of hard work in the city. The babies and children slept too, lulled by the drone of the engine. The driver had put up his hammock in the bus and slept while it was in the station, before it left; now he sat in the sole corona of light up front, beneath the *Ana Maria, Te amare x siempre* in white plastic letters above the top part of the windshield and the pale blue knitted baby shoes and gold crucifix dangling from the rear-view mirror.

Ismael had felt the music blaring through the slump of the brown vinyl bus seats, but now it was turned off. Beside him, Jose leant against the armrest, his head dangling out into the aisle of the bus like a toy on a coiled metal spring, the constant animation of his face and dimples evaporated by sleep, both hands laid atop his copious belly.

Ismael could not sleep. He opened the blacked out

window a crack and watched the potholed highway speed away from beneath them, a pitted boulder balanced on the brink of the road where it fell away. Leaning out, Ismael saw the waving stone of a ravine, bulging and ebbing, rushing down. He felt along the lines of the tender scars on his chest with a stumpy forefinger, and his hands shaped into his sisters' name signs. Rosie-old, clenched fist up under the chin; Cristina-big, elbows away from the chest.

The bus turned off the main road and began to disperse its passengers; an old woman with a grey braid and a clever, alive face and her three pink plastic bags of clothes and food in front of a white corner store, wood posts painted a now-peeling orange; a teenage girl in a strapless bright blue dress banded with black that hung around her skinny body and her equally scrawny baby in its cracked plastic carrier in front of a small, round arena, banked by row after row of wooden benches; a youngish man, sensitive face bloated with drink and poisons, in a barren lot covered with twisted grasses.

Ismael began to recognize the terrain. There was the cemetery where they had once passed a Day of the Dead, with its central blue concrete altar and the orange pillar grave marker. And now there was Peto, where his parents had gone to press thumbs down onto official papers just before they died.

With a shock, Ismael watched the town of the fiesta go by. Through a side road, he saw the central square, crowded with Maya; in the city their numbers had been diluted by Mexicans. There was the dirt path hemmed in by buildings that he had run through on the way to the cantina.

Beside him, Jose stirred. As his eyes opened, he too recognized the town of the fiesta. He opened the window fully and he and Ismael looked out together as the bus left the town where Ismael had first seen La Princesa.

Above the bus, the stars kept secret watch. Ismael could not fit the feeling they gave him into his mind. He had tried harder to contain the impression before the green-eyed woman, he realized.

Now that he was away from the city and beginning to condense the time in which she had dominated his life, Ismael did not push down so hard on the memory of her. She was like a movie star; hypnotizing and far removed. In spite of the pain and anguish that remained in him, Ismael carried a kernel of pride that he had her marks on his body, that someone as foreign as she had been so critical in his life.

As the bus neared home, he felt himself regaining the control he had enjoyed in the village. Already, he knew what he would tell the others about his time in the city, the signs he would choose, the emphasis that the punctuation marks of his facial expressions would give to points in the story.

He was rising above the unfiltered emotions and sensations that had flocked around him in the city, nipping at his ankles, receding and advancing without warning, tugging and pitching, pushing him below as forcefully and demandingly as the tides. Language would make a moat separating him from that primal, ancient wilderness again, and he would be an island. Not as much of one as the speaking people, but an island.

He was unquestionably glad to be returning to his privileged position next to Jose in front of the biggest store in town, passing tidy verdict on woes and miseries. Yet he knew he would experience a distance from his feelings, in the same way that a former user does from intoxication.

But he would be next to Rosie again, and Rosie would always live in that state. He resolved to be better to her.

Outside the window of the bus, the cornfields dipped into a hollow, and Ismael knew that hollow; he had planted seeds in it since he was a child, first next to his father and the grandfather who had died on the road outside town, and later next to Jose. He had once caressed the sides of Neidi's body there when they were young. Then they passed a tree Ismael had carved a circle into and suddenly he knew every ditch and plant in the panorama outside the bus.

The green sign with the bent corner and white lines on it that signified the village came up in front of them.

The bus stopped by the basketball court and the up-turned stones brought out from the ruins in the jungle. You could see the clean surfaces and edges, and know that they had been made with deliberation. The stones were the few fragments with pieces of hair, fists and bodies carved on them that hadn't been taken away by anonymous looters.

Ismael grasped his numerous plastic bags tightly as he followed Jose to the front of the bus, down the few steps, and onto the packed dirt road of his village.

An unfamiliar brown dog, its left eye a ball of sodden red, lay curled up in the centre of the basketball court, soaking in a pool of the blaring artificial light.

—Me forefinger-straight over there, Ismael told Jose. He wanted to go home on his own. Jose understood and extended his smooth, hairless arms; Ismael stayed thankfully in them for some moments before Jose turned past the old playground and the stone bench, through the earthy light that drove the shade into huddles on either side of the road. Past the store opposite the house with a drawing of a blue cow on it was Jose's sprawling complex of lean-tos and concrete squares, and there his smiling, buxom wife would be waiting impatiently in the matrimonial hammock.

Ismael walked straight ahead. Past the Catholic church on the left, doors now shut to the night; Ismael imagined the Virgin of Guadalupe sleeping in her nimbus of flames. On the right was the mint-green primary school, and next to it the medical clinic, and its back wall where he had met the girls of the village. As he walked by the houses, dark except for the weak glow of televisions escaping beneath the door and through the windows, he summoned up who was asleep in each.

The couple that lived in the house on the corner between their house and the primary school was crazy and childless. Nobody was sure whether the craziness or the childlessness had come first. Anyway, the words were synonymous.

The husband ran the small shop in the centre of the village that was open odd hours and was the shop that the drunks sat in front of. He also had a few video game machines and some boxes of candy and soda in a hut in front of his house. If you bought something from him and lost track of how much it was that you had given to him, he did not give you the change. He sat in his plastic chair with his hands on his fat knees, spread wide. His eyes did not see you even if you smiled to show him that you knew he was there.

The wife rolled around on the floor, her entire body

vibrating with laughter. She lifted her head momentarily and pointed a finger as big and crusty as a carrot at the ridiculous spectacle of you before the cackles and chortles overtook her again. Sometimes her tongue crept out of her mouth and hung there. She leapt on small things that nobody else talked about; you laughed, but then it did not stop.

Remembering them, Ismael repopulated his world. No more the pear-shaped old woman who had given him his Nescafé and chilaquiles in the big city, no more the armless, legless beggar with the face like a child's toy.

Then he was outside his house. He saw the black rope to the left of the front door that one could yank on the rare occasion that all three of them had been away and forgotten the key on its few links of chain with the straw hat dangling from it, and there was the patch of rust edged in white on the blue metal front door, and as he walked up the concrete steps he saw the scribbled lines that Cristiano from next door had put there.

Rosie and Cristina would be watching television still in the back room, Cristina constantly changing position in her hammock and swinging back and forth, hitting Rosie as she did. He would stick his hand through the horizontal shutters, always dusty, and signal to them to open the door; they would be able to see the movement in the other room and come to the door. They would recognize his hand straight away.

But when he put his hand through, nobody came. Ismael waved again and again. Maybe they had both fallen asleep. They would have had to do more work because he was not there. He imagined Rosie having to cut down food for the cows every day and his heart expanded in his chest, but he was here now and he would do it again, and she could rest.

He yanked on the black rope and the door yielded. He entered the front room with its large framed photograph of their grandparents and a cousin, the creases smoothed out. The three of them, Grandfather and cousin standing and Grandmother sitting on a stool in front of them, stared at the camera with bewilderment in their eyes. They did not know they were supposed to act like they knew everything would be all right. Ismael's shoulders dropped at seeing the photo; he was back home.

But there was no one in the back room. The television was off. He peered into the small beige room; only one hammock hung from wall to wall in it, and walking closer, he saw that Rosie's spongy shape was contorted into a ball, head down under her arms like a turtle, arms tightly wrapped around her midsection, knees under arms. He had never seen her sleep that way; always she lay much more loosely. He wanted badly to see her face, but did not want to force her out of the asylum of sleep.

Cristina must be sleeping in his room. Devious Cristina! He laughed to himself, easing back into being the patriarch. The foggy world simplified back into definition again, and as soon as it did, Ismael forgot that it had been different in the city. What else had Cristina done? She would have to go back into the room with Rosie tomorrow night. The yellow wooden door into his room always stuck just a bit, but he pushed on it and it scraped past the corner of the frame and into an empty room. Stale cigarette smoke smothered him. He had never smelled that odour in the house his parents had originally built. He scrabbled all around the four walls of the room in the dark for his hammock hung against the wall, but it was not there. Walking into the lean-to, he felt around for a hammock again and again did not find one. Would he sleep in the room with Rosie? But Cristina would need her hammock. She must be helping someone with a sick child; she would be back.

Exhaustion smashed down on Ismael as the adrenaline escaped him to gather on the floor like a steaming puddle of piss that heightened the miserable smell in the house.

He went back into his room, cleared some of the dust from the floor with his foot, spread clothes from his backpack onto it, and lay down like a dog to sleep. It was not how he had imagined his first night back home.

As he straightened his cramped body into the first grey light of the morning, the restorative smell of the cooking fire brought him into the day. Rosie was in the lean-to, her back to him, adding sticks to the orange smoulder and rapidly crumbling grey ash. A few long, anticipatory steps and he was behind her, reaching down to her shoulder. Spinning around, her eyes brightened. Her face was craggier, the nose more prominent, the lips thinner than Ismael remembered, and he saw that a deeper confusion shaded the trusting eyes. It brought him back into the time immediately before he had left, and the way that night at the fiesta had spread onto her body. Their separation had allowed him to pretend that she had been able to wash it away; the first sight of her eyes relieved him of that fiction, and told him that something irreversible had happened while he was away.

He spread his arms open and she went into them. He smelled her unchanged smell of sweat and woodsmoke, and beneath it the scent of a root vegetable straight out of the earth. When he drew back, she turned away fast and fell to her knees to cower by the fire, her eyes fixed on the flicker.

Ismael stroked her back. Rosie, Rosie, Rosie; her trust was a frail thing, but had he lost it already, after all those years by her side? She did not turn around but stayed on her haunches by the fire, nursing and comforting it as he now longed for her to nurse him. He knelt by her for a long while. An elegant, slender grey cat with bright green eyes purred against his thick calf, and he realized it was the kitten that had been near death when he left the village. So it had lived.

He went to retrieve the pink shawl he had bought her from his bags. Rosie smiled as she wrapped it around herself, and afterwards she turned to him again, but only momentarily.

Walking into the house, he opened the door into the sisters' bedroom. Cristina never slept much longer than this, and he was impatient for a trace of the imaginary exultant homecoming that had sustained him all those months lonely and alone in the city.

The room was empty, and so was his bedroom.

—Rosie-old, Rosie-old, where Cristina-big? Flat palm all around, forefinger wave, tell me where? Palm against forehead, palm against belly – forefinger wave, someone sick? Finger across neck, eyes turned up, tongue creeping out, someone dead?

She shrugged and stared at the fire. He could not stop himself from grabbing her shoulders and turning her to look at him.

—Rosie-old, where Cristina-big? Tell me now where Cristina-big.

As had been his way at home in the village, Ismael had not put a shirt on when he woke up. He did that only after breakfast, when he washed and got ready for the coming day. Rosie's eyes dropped to the two red parallel lines on his chest, the same painful length. The marks spread in her mind and the question grew in her eyes, against the panic Ismael had seen appear in response to his question about their sister's whereabouts.

He grabbed a shirt out of the nearest plastic bag and put it on over the scars.

The smoking logs of the fire contracted and startled him; it was a scorpion, crawling out of the depths of the fire and the boughs where it had taken shelter. He realized Rosie was looking at it too, and stepped to grab it in the same way he had the scorpion in that far-away room in the city where he had been stabbed. Here was his chance to get his sister to remember the way things had been before he left and the way things would be again. Something in the house had disintegrated. Cristina had been too preoccupied with herself to keep it together, but he would soon have everything right where it was wrong.

His flat foot with its cracked heel and the toes spread wide landed next to the scorpion and his broad hand reached for it, but its skeletal, bitterly black legs emerged between the fingers of his hand and tickled him as it clambered nimbly over him and scurried under the wall of the lean-to. Rosie watched it go, resignation in every fibre of her body.

Ismael left the house through the lean-to, angrily striding towards the centre of town. The two thick worms on his chest came alive again. He could feel a weight that hadn't been there before the woman and the scars.

Juan-Deafy with the horn around his neck was ahead of him on the road. When he turned his head to see who it was coming up behind him and realized that it was Ismael, the morning tiredness left his face and he ran to Ismael.

—Where you, where you, long long time! All wonder, where you! Me so happy see you!

Ismael forgot the hazy danger of the scorpion and the scars. The villagers swarmed around him, the children playing on the outskirts of the crowd, and beyond the children the dogs lay on the ground, tongues lolling. Past the dogs, the cornfields rolled into flaxen oblivion interrupted by knobbly trees, but Ismael did not look out there into the unknown any longer. He was in the very centre again. He felt returned home now, returned to himself, to his ability to make sense of things. He stuffed the words back down even as he signed them, and they stifled the last of the hot coals in his stomach, the last of the apparitions and the nameless dread. The noose of fervour that had hung above his head since the night of the fiesta settled down to burn steadily into its own death.

He was rounding his arms into a description of the woman in the city who had signed as beautifully as Jose when Ardrogna tunnelled through the throng as if following a faint reflux of vitality meandering through the rubbish of the group, and her ungainly, warty face came up right in front of Ismael.

—Ismael-strong, Ismael-strong! Sisters yours two crazy! Much much crazy, more crazy there time-past. Cristina-big, me see her walk over there jungle night time . . . thick thick jungle she in there. What she do? What she do, in there alone her? She crazy! Rosie-old, much distance everyone. Lonely alone her own push all away.

Ismael made one hand into the Pac-Man hand shape with its mouth open and closed it abruptly.

—Shut up.

It was the way he had always dealt with Ardrogna, and when she slunk away, it was some consolation for the failure of his attempt to destroy the scorpion.

As he went back into describing the deaf woman in the city, his mind was moving around the new knowledge of Cristina in the jungle in the middle of the night. Undergrowth, loamy soil, dark green, glistening leaves sagging with moisture and humidity, inch-long roaches scrambling from beds of decaying vegetation, and sweaty limbs prodded their way around and through the information. Nobody in the village went to the jungle in the night, and in the daytime, not even the men went on their own. As long as he had been away from his sister, Ismael still felt her, and he felt that the sparks that prickled at her and made her hungry would be stifled in the immensity and the sensation of the jungle, but she would not have gone out there by herself. Was it a secret lover? But who would want Cristina? And why would they need to meet at that hour, all that way outside of town, when in the daytime they could use the pale pink wall at the back of the schoolhouse or the small, ramshackle clinic at the edge of the village? Was it to see her ex-husband Antonio? Ismael had seen Cristina look longingly at Antonio, but he was married again and was happy.

Rosie knew everything, but she would never tell him.

The news that Ismael was back spread fast through the village, and the multitude shifted and reformed as people came and went for a glimpse of him and the stories that he had brought back. The sun moved through the sky and dawdled straight above for a longer time than usual, so that the day felt opened out, bigger. The villagers studied Ismael's face and remembered again how his eyes lay against the balance of his prominent nose and the wavering lines of his wrinkles. His eyes held the same blend of mischief and kindness, and they knew the lively smile. But Ismael had always met them with an unvarying solidity, no matter what they put to him, and now it had been ruptured.

Ismael told his stories with a new belligerence, his eyes darting from face to face and not resting anywhere. His walk was now a slightly lopsided shamble. His hands were floppier when he signed. Distraction had poked its way through his eyelids and dribbled into his eyeballs to join the mischief and kindness.

They saw it and they wondered at what had happened to him. They asked, but they knew his answers were not honest.

But his stories were entertaining. They needed diversion, and he needed to tell them.

So they crowded around: the tailor Chabelo, his unchanged beady eyes as eager as ever for news; ruddy Ramon, who had been ill while Ismael was away and lost weight; the reformed Estevanya, without the ribbons of black eyeliner going out to her hairline and now in a long, gauzy dress pulled over her round pregnant belly; Cristiano from next door, lengthened into the very beginnings of adolescence. Juan-Deafy stayed throughout the day, occasionally squeezing the horn that lay around his neck in his excitement, to the annoyance of those who could hear. The rebuffed Ardrogna winched her mountainous butt into a plastic chair and licked her chapped lips with expectancy. Cristobal, who had been a baby when Ismael left, was now a toddler already strutting with machismo. The crazy couple were both in their doorway and they were watching Ismael sneeringly. Jose ran back and forth to the store, keeping Ismael supplied with cold Coca-Colas in plastic bottles and later, with beer, as he swerved and braked and started up again on his way from story to story, enhancing and sub-tracting.

Ismael had been waiting to see Neidi, with her flat feet always shoeless, Neidi who made him laugh, but she did not appear.

Finally the sun stopped peering hungrily down at the squat form of Ismael in the middle of all the village and the heat lessened into easiness.

Rosie swayed past the group, her red plastic tub of corn kernels on her head, on the way to feed them through the grinder for corn dough to make tortillas with. She turned her head to her brother, back where he belonged, and the space in Ismael's heart that had emptied at her welcome of him that morning filled again when she smiled big and happy at him for a moment.

Then she turned her head abruptly back to the ground between her feet as she added one step onto another, the distance from where she had started accumulating, the place she wanted to go to and that she would be in very soon growing closer and closer, nothing else existing for her.

Ismael watched her for a time; and he too stood in the narrow, claustrophobic box of the present. Then he began to tell them about the bullfight he had gone to in the city, and the story pushed the sides of the box out.

Chapter Eleven

*I*smael back Ismael back Ismael back.
Ismael different now.

Before Ismael-strong, now Ismael-scar. Stab-chest finger through hand there heart shape. Finger-scar two. Ismael-scar that him.

Ismael-scar mind there scar. In chest all break both hands wave bottom chest, fizz fizz rise rise fall rise fall bottom chest hands stay long time then up again.

Me Rosie-old me see. Brush-away scar out mind, brush-away brush-away scar out body want.

Me Rosie-old me afraid close Ismael now. Try try think big strong tree but remember other prickly sharp spiky tree. Thorns same knife make scars. That why.

Tired not want here me Rosie-old me not want here no more.

The blood had come into Rosie's nose-holes when she was by Ismael.

She was happy to see him and to have his familiar broad body near her in the house. She had felt him there when she crouched by the fire, when she had dragged the orange plastic rake through the rocks and trash of the courtyard that morning.

But she saw now that not much had changed inside herself with Ismael's return. She washed the dishes, then sat in the green plastic chair and watched television for a while, and she watched people coming and going on the road out front from inside and not from outside on the steps. She did not see faces, only the jostle. She drew the pink shawl Ismael had given her tighter around herself, as she could not draw his presence around herself.

The scorpions came from under the walls, out of the fire, creeping along the roof of the house, falling onto the floor of the kitchen to thrash blackly. They were knotted to the change in the atmosphere, and their presence choked Rosie. She did not know how to untie the knot, and she did not try to stop them. She knew now that Ismael could not.

The fan stirred the stagnant air of the house, and Rosie sat directly in front of it. The currents of the air made a harmony that played over her skin and transported her. She drew lines with her finger on the dusty blades of the fan and fixed her eyes on the lines until the fan spun too fast and she lost them, lost them like the life she had known how to exist in.

The tops of her bare feet puffed up like tortillas when you tapped their centres to see if they were ready. The scorpions tickled her when they ran over her feet, and Rosie wished for their sting.

She remembered when the burros had run through here, trotting in a lively way. She and Ismael were small, before Cristina was born. The stubby Mohawks of the burros defied those who had stood outside their pole houses with the palm-frond roofs, watching the grey spectres hurtle past and off into the trees.

Then one day you had to step over the gassy-swollen bodies of the burros to walk to the store or to the church come a Sunday. The odour of putrid flesh drenched the village. The town became a graveyard of bones and the children draped sheets over the burro ribcages and played mama-and-papa beneath. Finally, the women swept away the last of the bone chips and the burros were forgotten. They never came back.

Ardrogna peered through the horizontal shutters of the window and interrupted Rosie's recollection of that other critical time.

Rosie turned the handle that closed the shutters. The pointy tip of Ardrogna's nose stuck for a few seconds between two shutters and reddened before she twisted it free.

The long dusty road into the jungle stretched slightly uphill from the centre of the town where Ismael and the others stood. If you followed it, you passed the log raised between two forked sticks that marked the old well which Ismael had looked into on his long walk back to the village after killing the man. A flat rectangular rock half-covered the cavity. The grandmothers of the villagers had once walked back and forth to the well daily, to get water to cook with.

And beyond the well was the high rock pile that was all that was left of the temple. At the bottom was the inactive volcano.

There was a piece of frayed yellow rope tied to a tree a short way up the rock pile, and Neidi grabbed hold of it so it could help Cristina take the first step down. Rocks came loose and went falling down the pile. Neidi wedged her bare foot against a gnarled root and took another step below to the next rock that seemed secure. Above her, Cristina's bottom was large in its tight blue and yellow flowered skirt and her white plastic sandals, the ones she had got from their cousin for her birthday, slipped, pebbles tumbling down to hit Neidi, and then found a foothold against the base of a tree as she crawled to the bottom, hand and foot.

Behind them was the mouth of what people said was the volcano, but there was no glimmer at the bottom to give them a sense of what had been down there. Cristina did not look down it for long.

Many uncountable years before, when the volcano had last erupted, there had not been any humans in the area around. It erupted, it caused change, and then there was rebirth.

Now the fermenting provocations at the bottom of the volcano, at the heart of the earth, drifted up and entered the people in the village nearby, and became emotions, and all that happened after that was opaque.

Cristina extended one foot, feeling beneath her. Her hands made grooves in Neidi's wet, perspiring shoulders as Cristina clamped onto them, lowering her tubby legs in their flip-flops to land heavily onto a rock that held firm. They each had one leg on the same flat rock, Cristina and Neidi; Neidi's gaunt calves, the stringy meat sagging from the brittle bone, next to Cristina's burly ones covered in rough stubble. Above their legs, their egg-shaped bodies were more similar, and in the centres of their bodies, their hearts now beat with the same rhythm.

Beneath the black at the bottom of the volcano, beneath the deadness, the magma pulsated and it harmonized with their heartbeats, with the blood in their veins, with the agitation in their bellies. They did not know what it was or where it came from, but they felt it, and they stayed there on the rock. A light sweat came out across their upper lips.

They had awakened in the hut together, bodies pressed

close in the hammock, but closed their eyes to the day and light coming through the palm fronds.

Cristina told Neidi still more secrets: about her grandfather, how he had beat her grandmother and her father had beat her mother, and she had seen everything but never told anyone, and there were many more secrets; her life was a tragic song that no one knew, but which she needed to tell Neidi. Neidi did not know what there was to say, only that she did not see these phantoms Cristina wanted to introduce her to. She could only take Cristina into her arms again.

Finally the day found them, and towed them along after it.

Beyond Neidi's damp, greenish skin with tiny pinpricks in it below the eye-bags, beyond the living bones propping the face up, her mind had been happy to let the day lead it, but now it struggled up and away on its own, and it thought that she and Cristina had to go back to the village now. How had it gotten so late? How had they forgotten the conditions and situations of their lives?

—We go back now, Neidi told Cristina. Her finger searched its way down from the heights and mapped their way back to the village. Her other hand rounded and became the buildings that they needed to return to.

Now Neidi took her foot off the flat rock and walked

all the way to the bottom of the rock pile, and from there to the well. They did not look down the dark hole as Ismael had. And from the well to the road. Cristina kept her eye on the centre of Neidi's flaccid back and the round of sweat that widened between her shoulder blades. The uneven pebbles and brown, mouldering vegetation of the jungle became the hard road, and the red soil clouded around their feet with each step, and the sun and the earth pressed together onto Cristina and Neidi as they had not in the jungle. Cristina walked alongside Neidi and not behind her. Their left legs swung out, and then their right; their calves wobbled as their feet landed on the ground, the pebbles of the road stinging Neidi's shoeless feet as they slapped up and down. Their arms came up across their chests with each step. It had originally been Cristina who walked like this, whilst Neidi's arms stayed by her sides, but without noticing it, Neidi now mirrored Cristina.

A chicken ran on the road in front of them, taking short, stiff steps, its beady eyes gleaming. Chicken, finger-beak pecking in front of nose.

A hog trotted by on its four stubby legs, two tusks of whitish-pink tissue wobbling from under its jaw. Hog, four fingers of the hand held on top of the nose and flapping downwards, like the slimy diagonal of the pig's snout.

Trees lined the road. Tree, forearm as the trunk, fingers

pointed towards the sky, hand moving to represent the living stuff that flickered inside of these stationary creatures.

Cristina did not think of her grandmother or of the grandfather who had pulled himself painfully along this same road and started the developing intensity that had brought her here, beside Neidi. Agony and the past had been expelled. She had found the way she would live without Ismael, and she felt that she lived more fully than she had when he was around, in the world of flesh again as she had thought she never would. After the years of eating, sleeping, watching television, cleaning, and cooking alongside her brother and sister, and of struggling to keep the smouldering in her stomach from catching fire, she felt freed from the days. She had a new, robust impression of the semblance of life, and it occupied her fully. She did not have room to see how she had painfully affected Rosie, who had no way to go on now.

Beside her, Neidi was more cautious. She had gone years with one eye keeping watch, but during the last few weeks with Cristina she had been indolent. She watched her feelings slither into the world and alter it for her as they became concrete things, and then enter into her again to breed and transmute. She thought she could see Cristina's feelings do the same, as she had never before seen anyone else's. The colours, design, and textures of Cristina's were different from her own. Neidi studied them with care, as one would study the patterns on butterfly wings, and her earlier diligence was forgotten. Now it returned with a brusque snap. She was thinking that when they got closer to the village, she would walk further away from Cristina, that she would say they had ranged further than usual whilst cutting down food for the cows and had got lost in the jungle. She would not look at Cristina as she explained, and she would not meet Cristina in the night again for many months.

Their wet limbs moved parallel to each other; their mournful brown eyes looked straight ahead, Cristina's squinty and small, Neidi's large and droopy. Their skin, well scoured by time and heat, met the sun yet again.

The road sloped gently downwards and they neared the village. Trees gave way to buildings; first the large white square of the older children's school, with the wire fence around it, and then the houses. A face peeked out from behind the horizontal shutters of a window, as if from behind bars, and Neidi walked still further out front from Cristina, striding fretfully.

The village was strangely deserted. There was no one in the stores they passed, not even behind the counters, and no children dragged toys on string through the streets.

Outside the church, the priest had dragged the aluminium ladder over from the side where they usually kept it and leant it against the tree, and then he climbed the ladder slowly, gripping rung after rung with one hand as he held the shears in the other. When he was at the top, he used the clippers ferociously on the branches, severing even the ones that didn't need to be cut away. His mouth worked in time with the shears, his top and bottom jaw meeting hard as the metal of the shears snapped.

Cristina and Neidi went beyond the store opposite the house with a drawing of a blue cow on it, and below them was the basketball court, and in the court was a mob, everyone from the village sucked into it.

Cristina looked uncomprehendingly at it. The only time the village gathered in the basketball court was for a holiday or a fiesta, and she knew today was neither. They must know about her and Neidi; they must be waiting to crack down on them, like the priest's clippers decimating the plants.

She turned to run back into the jungle. In her mind was an image that had come to her again and again as she lay in her hammock in the night, before she had started meeting Neidi in secret. It was a thin arm waving at her with a regular pulse, through layers of hot fire. The way the long, narrow fingers were bent and then unbent asked Cristina hungrily for something.

Neidi would not let her turn back.

—Stay here behind me, we finger-walk, finger-walk

down there eyes-see all people. Calm calm. When reach square-court there, you go left that way finger-point, me go right that way finger-point. Calm calm Cristina-big, calm calm.

Cristina dropped back again as Neidi told her to. She kept her eyes on the ground, tried to banish the remembrances of the arm waving from fire and the priest chomping his clippers violently down onto the plants.

But something was coming down on their ignorant if not innocent heads, she felt it. Cristina was ensnared, they all were, and it would not stop now. Cristina did not know why, yet she knew it to be true.

A good-looking male body encased in bright green entered the lower border of her eyesight. She knew the straight configuration of the wide chest. It was Ismael.

He turned and he looked at her, edging into the left periphery of the crowd as Neidi did the same on the far right.

She smelled it in him and on him, the change and the blood. Some people always looked the same, and were the same. Ismael had been one of those people, but no longer. And he was secreting himself in the shifting crowd and stories, as if it could be that easy.

He knew the change in her with no less force, and he saw the reason where she did not for him. He glared at her.

A steely prod into the small of her back pushed her to him, and the cavernous, edgy eyes of the village watched as Cristina stumbled forward to grasp Ismael between her arms for a long moment.

Herman who worked in the big store was slaughtering a cow. Cristina saw it as she turned away from Ismael, hoping that the intoxication of telling his stories to the village would absorb him for a little longer. Long enough for her to understand that he was back.

The claret blood of the cow that lay gashed open seeped into the hard-packed earth. Mottled purple striated over firm pink offal collapsed on the dirt like a collection of marbles. Milky blubber lay under the bristle and above the variegated ligament beneath which bone showed itself in places, and the ebony hooves lolled gracelessly apart, and the useless ivory horns lay above the dull eye.

Cristina took in the raw, florid flesh with a restless gaze. The spectacle exorcized the demons that had reappeared in her upon seeing Ismael. It was the Holy Communion of Christ's blood and flesh, stripped of high-minded symbol. But without the demons a draught passed straight and freezing through the resurrected gaps in Cristina, so she reached out for them again to wrap around herself like a scratchy, cheap cloak.

The rich, substantial whiff of blood came to her again,

intensified, and now she glanced at the carcass. The meat, the bone, the viscera, ossifying, and the smell of blood on her brother.

She pulled herself up out of her stunned state on the rope of the smell, and into immediacy; but some of the smell and meat stayed with her, as if seeing Ismael again had reduced things to their barest reality. The amplified life of the months he had been gone, when everything had seemed brighter or darker, flattened again.

Neidi had integrated herself into the crowd, Cristina saw. She stood with Juan-Deafy and his basket of *chicharrones* and hot sauce, her black eyes sparkling as the hands Cristina knew so well offered up some crumb of talk to Juan-Deafy. Cristina felt that their long, languorous hours in the jungle should have overlaid some shining, spiderweb pattern of need onto Neidi's face and body, and protected her from what she sensed was coming with Ismael's arrival; but Neidi appeared the same as she always had. Cristina wondered if she herself did also.

Ismael had finished his story, and his changed, castigating eyes were fully on Cristina now.

Again she thought of going back into the jungle, but Ismael would find her wherever she went. The reek of antagonism had reached her from many places, but it was strongest when it came from her brother. It had never come from Rosie. She suddenly realized that nothing at all came to her from Rosie. She had always felt her sister's firm, quiet presence; but it was gone from the atmosphere.

Her hand went up and the fingers turned inwards as she beckoned to Ismael to follow her back to the house. She wanted to know exactly what was happening. And there were leftover lentil and ground pumpkin seed empanadas, the dish Ismael loved best.

Inside the house, they looked at each other, Ismael, Cristina, and Rosie. Each was elementally different to when they had last been together.

Between them elongated a stain of filth and carelessness that reached towards all three with equal accusation, and somehow had their grandmother at the centre. Their eyes, separately, considered.

Ismael demanded, pointing to Cristina,

—What you do, what you do, think self self me me!

The ashes in the banked fire in her stomach came alive again. They went wriggling up Cristina and ulcerated. Everything that Ismael had left them with, the questions and the explanations and the unearthing they had had to do because he had abandoned them, and the feelings he had set off flickering through their bodies, hers and Rosie's, all of it compressed and forced into these small, petty words now.

—What you do!

And she was supposed to give him an answer.

Cristina swallowed gastric juice back down and turned away from Ismael.

He reached out, stout with complete certainty, and grabbed her shoulder, turning her towards him again.

Cristina gave back to Ismael,

—Me cook cook you, me work work much, clean house, you sneak rat much us not know! Who that green-eyed woman there fiesta? What happen you gone? Why stay stay long time?

They stood and stared at each other, and through Cristina's resentment came gratification at seeing her brother again, at having his sloping shoulders that had held up so much for his sisters in the house. It was replicated in her brother's disillusioned eyes and if it was allowed to come into bud they might have a chance of going on, Cristina thought. It was more than many bloodless people in the world had. But neither Ismael nor Cristina allowed it to stay long enough.

Between them, Rosie sat in her rubber chair, holding an orange segment up to the light from the bare bulb hanging in the middle of the ceiling. The world was made golden through the luminous wedge of orange. Rosie put more pieces of orange, spurting sweet and brilliant, into her mouth, but she did not take her eyes off her prism.

—Me smell you different, Cristina told Ismael.

—You different. What different?

Her two fists came up to her heart and pressed together, then broke apart.

—Something is broken in you, she told Ismael.

Ismael pointed at her and put a palm held sideways in the air behind his back, brought it forwards to stop in front of his chest, then he put both fists together in front of his heart to break apart, in the same way that Cristina had. Now he pointed at the ground at his feet and made the breaking sign again, but his motion was stronger, more violent.

—You have always been broken, but now you are even more broken, he said to his sister.

Around them, the world was the same as it had always been. The maggots and beetles had retreated, there were no scorpions in the house. The sky was a supple blue and the pointed fringes of the palm trees moved gently in the air. There was a new litter of kittens in the house across the street, and the children knelt by them, curiously examining the unseeing, cloudy eyes and the mewling pink mouths.

But the territory within was always changing, and it coloured the world as surely as Rosie's orange held up to the light.

Where did the skeleton of the thing lie? Nobody knew. Something that knew everything was in the centre of the room, between the three of them, in the midst of the filth and carelessness. It was ravenous and ready to snatch down onto the smallest bit of flesh. Its scent was too faint for them to detect, but there were layers of lush, putrefied egg above stale, yeasty alcohol.

And the angels and seraphs that had come to Ismael in his red hammock up on the mountain above the city and enriched him did not come to him in this place he had returned to.

Rosie lowered the orange from her eye and the world stopped being golden. Again she saw the dirt creeping out of the doorways of the house, the dirt that she had tried so hard to control. There were splotches and holes where the paint had chipped off and the grey, rough concrete showed through. Scratches made a halo around the holes. Skid marks of the red dust scattered over the floor. It blew through the glassless windows all day long and Rosie could not sweep it all away; it came back fast. The tops of the framed pictures were coated with it, and the Holy Bible they had been given by the missionary. The chip of pure glass hung on a ribbon that made rainbows on the wall when the sun shone through it was now encrusted with dirt. Their young faces in Rosie's favourite picture had become smudged and could not be seen clearly any longer.

She could not see Ismael's or Cristina's face as they

stood in front of her either, she thought. Their features had folded into a viscous blur, one much the same as the other.

She was tired to the bone; she could not try to keep things intact any longer.

She had thought that they could; that their mysterious words and signs outlined things and kept them configured, that they would be able to see each other faintly once they were in the same place again.

She got to her feet. The soft, cottony, starless dark had come, and it would seal her eyes against the fear. She would walk through it to the big store to get flour tortillas and slices of ham, and nothing would be able to touch her, see her, smell her, try to explain her, for those few minutes.

A few pesos shining through the fingers of her clenched fist, Rosie opened the door of the house and carefully placed first one foot and then the other on the first step and the second, and on the road.

As she took precise steps along the road to the store, a small black truck with its headlights off sped hastily out of the passage between their house and the next. Her head turned slowly in the direction of the truck, and she saw it as it collided with her and she flipped onto the rocks in front of their house and the rocks embedded themselves in her forehead, the rocks beneath the cook-pots and plastic containers she had planted herbs in.

The smell of her blood blended easy and smooth with the other primeval smell that knew everything, and the blood saturated the yellow flowers she had embroidered across the top of her dress and it came richly into her mouth. The incandescence that she had always felt resting above the sky draped her in its warm, smooth lustre and she was allayed of everything.

She came back to the scene for a moment. People surrounded her. Rosie felt the presence there of Ismael and Cristina, and of course there was Ardrogna, and there was so much chatter on all sides.

Me Rosie-old me not like much dirt, much broken pieces. Better now. Clean, right on on on left on on on away calm calm now calm me Rosie me like calm.

She jerked and struggled in Cristina's arms before she went quiet.

Cristina watched her sister die, and she remembered the cow that morning, and the blood still on her brother. And again the demons were exorcized from her, but this time she did not draw the cloak around herself again.

Ismael and Cristina sat on their front stoop as twilight plummeted down onto them. It was a few months after the car accident.

Cristina watched as Ismael drew up his shirt and rubbed

the thick scars on his chest, as he always did at the end of the day. She did not think he knew that he did it. The scars were some of the first things she saw in the morning, and also last thing, when they sat together watching television before they went to bed. Often Ismael would take off his shirt in the heat of the day, like the other men in the village.

She did not ask him where the scars had come from, or what had happened to him while he was away, and he did not tell her. She did not know if he even allowed himself to remember it; she felt she would have been able to see the new expression on his face that these thoughts would make. She saw the buried split there in him every day, and she moved delicately around it. It was now a part of Ismael.

But she had taken away that tattered *Wey-yano'one* shirt that he had brought back from wherever he had been, stained with blood, and she had ripped it into rags.

Outside the village, the corn had been harvested and the fields lay bare and shorn. The stubble of the corn poked up pitiably, struggling to hide the nakedness.

Neidi came to visit Cristina every day, and Ismael did not say anything, but he told Cristina never to go out in the jungle again without him.

There were more scorpions than there had been before Ismael had left the village, more elemental discontent. They both saw it, and they saw each other seeing.

Ismael pumped his fist in and out; one day soon he would be able to reach down and crush them in his fist again, as he had not been able to for Rosie.

Her picture hung on the wall. Cristina squeezed cleanser on the glass and the surrounding frame every day, and wiped away the residue of the world from it. Rosie would be kept apart from all of it now.

Cristina crossed her plump calves on the step and remembered Rosie sitting above her on the step, plucking the white hairs from her head so she would be able to find another husband. She remembered how the bottom line of their thighs sagged in the same way, one on the step above the other.

Beside her, Ismael was counting the hours till the dark night would give way to the morning. The precious illumination had started to come to him again then.

He remembered their grandmother out on the road to the jungle, and their grandfather trying to crawl back to town and failing, and Rosie, dying here in the village.

He held up his hands and he made the sign for death. The finger across the neck, the eyes turned up, the tongue creeping out as something left the body. The expression on the face; the palms down by the waist, and sweeping away.

He felt Cristina's eyes on him. Neither of them understood more than they had and they had not done that much better or much worse than their grandparents.

But as he made the sign, he looked at his sister, culpable and vulnerable, and he knew the same things were coming together in both of them.

In the morning, the laughing wind came to both Ismael and Cristina and washed them clean to begin another day.

Acknowledgements

Thank you to the Kindle Project, the Society of Authors, the Authors' Foundation, Hawthornden Castle, Arts Council England, Jen Paige Macdougall, Gabriel Arellano, Hubert Smith, Robert Johnson, Shaheen Rassoul, Sadaf Rassoul Cameron, Zelda, Zebedee, Sam Taylor-Johnson, Majahua, Lupita, Venja and Pepe, Roberto, Tonio and Lisa, Francoise, familia Salamanca, Roger Ballen, Hannah Westland, Bella Lacey, Peter Straus and Max Porter.

And bless, bless to beloved friends and family as before and always.